PRAISE FOR BAFFLING YEAR ONE

"There are no false notes in this strange and dazzling anthology of 26 queer, speculative stories, selected from the first year of *Baffling Magazine*—which is particularly impressive given the wide range of tone, subject matter, and subgenre."

—Publishers Weekly (starred review)

Neon Hemlock Press
www.neonhemlock.com
@neonhemlock

Baffling Year Two
edited by dave ring, Craig L. Gidney & Gabriella Etoniru

Cover Illustration by Justin Lanjil
Cover Design and Layout by dave ring
Interior Harpy Illustrations by Robin Ha

Print ISBN-13: 978-1-952086-76-2
Ebook ISBN-13: 978-1-952086-77-9

edited by dave ring, Craig L. Gidney & Gabriella Etoniru
BAFFLING YEAR TWO

Neon Hemlock Press

Baffling
Year Two

EDITED BY DAVE RING
CRAIG L. GIDNEY & GABRIELLA ETONIRU

SPECULATIVE

FLASH

FICTION

WITH A

QUEER

BENT

ℭONTENTS

MEN AGAINST THE CURRENT

LOUIS EVANS

TWENTY-ONE YEARS Ambroso Garzolo had spent, after the death of his lover, looking for that other Venice— and without any apparent success.

Johann had been an earthy man, hearty and sensible, and so of course in his absence, without his counsel, Ambroso sought him through every excess of esotericism.

He followed every contradictory suggestion in a dozen ancient codices. He prayed. He fasted. He sponsored monasteries and ascetics. He took tinctures of potent spices. He worked gematria with kabbalists and sought wisdom with alchemists. He summoned spirits on the occasion of rare astrological conjunctions. He purchased saintly relics and profaned them. He drew the symbols of Hermetic magic on his floors in chalk and on his walls in blood and fire.

Nothing worked. After every rite and every ordeal, Ambroso always awoke to the same Venice, except he had become notorious, or wounded, or was in trouble with the law, his creditors, or the church. Not one experiment ever recovered a glimmer of Johann's smile, or hint of his perfume, let alone brought Ambroso to the other Venice.

Twenty-one years.

And then, tonight, he finds it without trying.

He steps out of the back of his palazzo onto his private quay and up above the sky is gone, replaced with a vast parchment, lit from within, an obscure branching diagram inscribed upon it in vast strokes of ink.

Though the pale sky suggests daytime, nevertheless the city, the other Venice, is immensely dark and cold. All the palazzos—and there are many, many palazzos, countless buildings of all kinds, two dozen at least for every edifice that stands in the Venice of living men—are in shadow, torches burning in their sconces to hold away the night. In the distance, interlocking inverted districts of the other Venice rise up at odd angles, as though the city herself sat not on a flat lagoon but instead on a sort of peculiar saddle-shaped hill; but Ambroso (born centuries before Escher or Gauss) cannot name the hyperbolic tessellation, and must simply note that the horizon is not exactly visible and in any case quite the wrong shape altogether.

The cold is so bitter that Ambroso's face and hands chap immediately. It is colder than he can ever remember, colder even than the midwinter day in his boyhood when all the canals froze. But the canals of the other Venice are not frozen. Something is moving in them, something that is not water; something odorless and dark and shining, neither blood nor ink.

The private quay is unchanged: a simple spit of fitted stone. The gondola at its end is just like any gondola that has ever passed Ambroso's window.

The gondoliere is a skeleton. He wears a traditional gondoliere's costume and a blindfold over empty eye sockets. Half his teeth are missing or chipped; his cheekbone has broken and healed. He makes no gesture, neither of invitation nor dissuasion, as Ambroso boards the gondola.

How else to travel, in any Venice?

Hands of bone push the pole through the liquid that is neither water nor quicksilver. The gondola glides out into the canal. For a long time they pass through branching paths in silence.

At last, Ambroso speaks. "Have I died?"

"Do dead men ask this question?" Which is much less than an answer. But independent gondolieri are quarrelsome and contradictory even in the living Venice; Ambroso knows better than to complain.

They pass the Piazza San Marco, where in life Ambroso Garzolo had first spied the burly Dutchman who would become king of his heart; his soul sings out with the memory.

They pass the Piazza San Marco *again*; but this time, the facade of the Biblioteca Marciana has been shattered by cannonfire. Suppurating holes march across its surface like buboes across a victim of plague. They pass the Piazza San Marco again, and now, instead of the basilica looming above, there is a Saracen minaret, such as the Turks have built beside the Hagia Sophia.

"So this is not the Venice of the dead," murmurs Ambroso, as if to himself. He is relying on the natural disposition of a quarrelsome man to correct another in his private thoughts; even when the quarrelsome man is a quarrelsome skeleton. "This is...the other Venice of...other Venices."

"The living Venice is a city of countless canals," says the skeleton. He, too, pretends he is talking to himself. "In my Serenissima they are countless *beyond* countlessness."

"Gondoliere?" asks Ambroso.

The skeleton spits nothing over the boat's edge.

"Can you take me to the Venice where Johann survives?" Some other Venice, quite nearby, where the fires of plague had on that fatal night *receded* and spared the man Ambroso had nursed like a baby and whose corpse he had subsequently wept over, rather than rising to an all-consuming peak and lifting his beloved's incinerated soul off to heaven.

"I can take you to any place you can point out."

But what good is this? The other Venice is devoid of life. No boats, no boatmen; no merchants, no monks; not even pigeons erupting from the Piazza San Marco, which they are passing again, only now the papal banner of the Borgias flies from the clocktower. Only the shimmering liquid over which they fly displays the barest sign of movement. How can Ambroso pluck a living Johann from this dead maze?

No matter. For the chance to lay a hand on Johann's arm for but a moment, Ambroso defies impossibility.

"Onward," he says, and onward they go.

Palazzo upon palazzo; church after church. Wondrous sights: a Roman amphitheater; the Arsenal expanded to colossal proportions with a massive Sumerian lamassu above its threshold; a nine-masted junk laying at anchor whose figurehead is a feathered serpent of hammered gold. Terrible sights also: bridges shattered, buildings sunk, palaces in wind-worn ruins.

Yet regardless of its condition, the empty city shows no sign of Johann. Hour by hour Ambroso's thoughts spiral toward despair.

Even if he *could* find a Venice where Johann lived, his happiness would be far from assured. Perhaps there would be another Ambroso there, to dispute possession; perhaps Johann would have departed for his homeland, or Brazil, or Macau, following his own wandering heart. Perhaps they would have broken from one another acrimoniously; and Ambroso's aged face would be hateful to this strange Johann.

Borne down by the weight of these forebodings on what had seemed the threshold of triumph, Ambroso slumps on his bench, defeated. He leans over the edge of the boat and looks down into what is not the water.

And there, in the blond-bearded, ruddy face looking up at him that is not his reflection, he finds what he had no hope of finding. The answer to his question: where do you find your lost beloved, for whom you have spent twenty-one long years searching?

You find him where he is searching for you.

Ambroso reaches out. His fingers enter the frothing darkness. Only Ambroso knows whether Johann's fingers, reaching back, brush against his own—and even he is uncertain.

"I cannot advise this," says the skeleton.

But Ambroso Garzolo is beyond advice. With only uncertainty to guide him, Ambroso goes over the side, into the beyond.

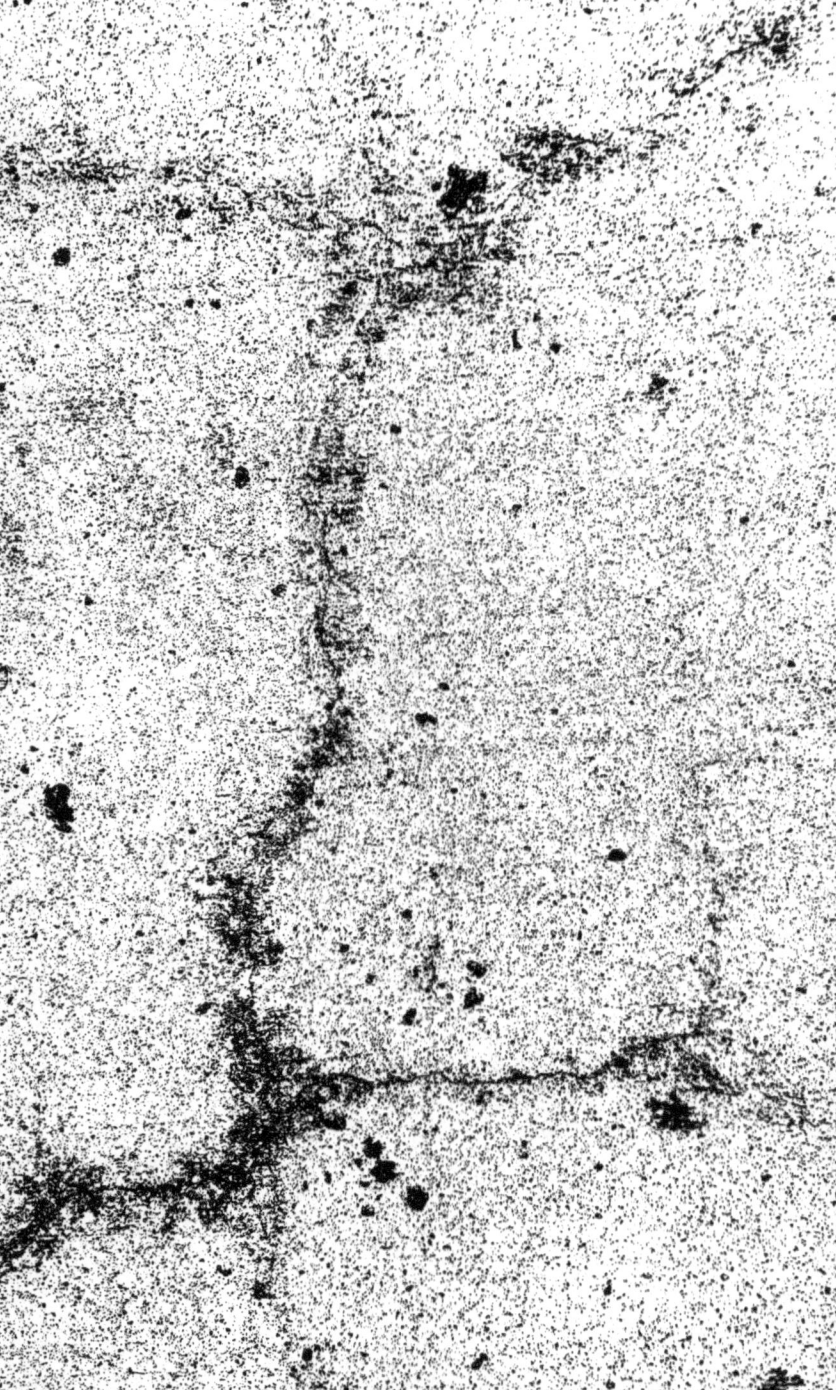

ONE AND A HALF STARS

KRISTEN KOOPMAN

EFORE ANYONE CONSIDERS buying this uterus, let me
share a little story.

Said uterus broke at three o'clock in the morning
on a Tuesday. The persistent error messages, better known
as cramps, woke me up faster and more viciously than any
smoke detector's ever managed. I guess I'm not the first
one to wonder why the technological marvel of our age
uses *cramps* instead a push notification, because here's a
quote from the company's FAQ: "The body already has
an alert system, so your artificial uterus interfaces with
your nervous system to alert you using the same methods
that a natural organ would."

I cannot articulate just how much my blood pressure
rose when I realized that the dull aching interspersed with
unpredictable shooting pains was a feature and not a bug.

By three-fifteen I had knocked out all the standard
uterine troubleshooting steps: I had forced a soft reboot
from my phone, run the automatic troubleshooting
program, updated the app, update the device software
(which is apparently different from updating the app), and
turned the external router off and on again. By three-

thirty I gave up, put on a pot of coffee, took a painkiller, and began searching variations of *why cramps WHY* on the website. Everything pointed to replacement, and no other options. The turnaround times and shipping costs on within-warrantee uterus repair, by the way, are *ridiculous*.

So I looked elsewhere, to no luck. What I *did* find were advice columns for post-implantation cramps, snippets of code for fetishists wanting to know how to hack the wetware, and list-articles like "You Won't Believe What People With Uteruses Had To Put Up With In The Olden Days!"

By five, the coffee was gone and I had re-read the entire user manual for my uterus four times. According to the manual, these error messages (again: excruciating pain) are always supposed to be accompanied by a notification in the app. According to my app, everything was business as usual, although nobody told that to the sluggish, red-hot knife "alerts" being swirled through my internal organs. The only exception to this error policy was supposed to occur when the uterus was in conception mode, being cleaned faster and more regularly until a fertilized egg implants. The muscle contractions that cause cramps are present for those monthly cleanings, unlike annual cleanings, because...why, exactly? They're not medically necessary either way. Who wrote that bit of code, the Pope? Originalsin.exe?

I'm getting off topic. At this point, it had become a matter of *principle*. I'm decently good with technology. I've got degrees. My generation grew up with this sort of thing. One uterus and some cramps: how hard could it be? I want convenience; I want consistency; I want ease; and more than any of that, I want to not be defeated by a goddamn artificial uterus.

But it's very hard, apparently, judging by the *three days* of Sisyphean forwarded calls, call-back waits, online chats, and even an in-person doctor's visit. (Expect a strongly worded follow-up from my gynecologist, by the way; she is *pissed*.) For 72 hours, because someone decided that pain was the most "natural" error message, my abdomen felt like someone had hung weights from my intestines so that every single motion would *yank* on them. All that, only to be told that it probably just needed a hard restart.

Want to know what a hard restart entails? Somewhere inside my pelvis a patch of plastic interfaces with the wetware, and that plastic has a small recessed button in it. The instrument to press that button is proprietary and the procedure is technically considered troubleshooting rather than medical intervention, so it isn't covered by my insurance—and after all the cease-and-desists sent to doctors who did it anyway, my gynecologist couldn't do it even if she wanted to. Instead, I'm supposed to pay out-of-pocket to wait in a Device Clinic to be seen within a four-hour window so some stranger without a medical degree can stick a special skewer up my hoo-ha.

Well, screw that.

I've done many intimate things with my partner. We've whispered postcoital secrets to each other, brushed our teeth on the toilet while the other showered, shared more bodily functions in each other's presence than anyone really wants to admit exists. We know each other's acne scars and birthmarks, have memorized every unhygienic habit and guilty pleasure, have smelled—well. Everything.

Nothing we have ever done has been as intimate or uncomfortable as when my partner spelunked my vagina with an unbent paperclip duct-taped to an old kabob skewer.

All to push a button that turns my uterus off and then on again.

So designers, when you come out with the flashy next model, here's a word of advice: use those nerves for something else. Anything else. You're smart. I'm sure you can figure out how to do pins-and-needles or (every gynecologist's favorite!) "slight pressure." Better yet, send the error messages to the app. That's what it's for, *right*?

In short, would not recommend. I give it half a star for uterine function. And one star for the built-in wifi hotspot.

MR. MARIGOLD RESHELLS AN AUTOMATON

ARDEN POWELL

𝕿HE AUTOMATON WAS not supposed to be conscious, but it looked around with inquisitive amber eyes. "I thought I was a shell."

So too had Mr. Marigold. "I intended to repurpose you," he confessed.

They were in the back room of his shop, myriad unfinished sculptures standing in the corners, his tools scattered across the table. Silver filigree and tight spools of bright copper wire waited to be spun into beauty. Dust motes drifted in the sunbeam that filtered through the tiny window in the roof, turning the room sepia.

"Are you going to make me into art?"

Mr. Marigold gave his moustache a thoughtful tug. "I've never met a self-aware automaton. It doesn't seem right to make the choice for you."

The automaton's bronze was dull and scratched from years of neglect, the gears that whirred within its chassis clunky and stuck with grime. "These are not my original parts." Disapproval coloured its tone as it ran halting fingers over its curves and edges. "These machinations are crude. Who made me into this?"

"I bought you off an old museum when they closed. You had been in storage for decades. No one remembered where you came from."

"Da Vinci built me. His design was imperfect, but he treated me as a person. After he died, they made me into a thing."

"Tell me how you want to look, and I'll make you into that."

The automaton pointed to two tiny sculptures whittled out of basswood, one male and one female. "Are those my options?" Its gaze returned to the length of its body. "Even Da Vinci made me more human than I wanted. He built me broad-shouldered and thick, like his Vitruvian Man."

"How, then, would you appear?"

"Beautiful. Like a minnow, or a bird in flight. I want to look like my own being."

Mr. Marigold built the automaton a new frame out of the lightest steel, and a shell of porcelain and ivory. At each step, he had to earn the automaton's trust anew, adapting to its reaction with every change he made. Every joint was articulated with loving attention, every line pared down to its sleekest and simplest design. When the automaton was finally pleased with its silhouette, Mr. Marigold swept in with his brushes, turning the slender figure into living art. Rococo patterns swirled over the porcelain in gold leaf and china blue. Swallows adorned its shoulders; florals twined over its limbs. The automaton sat on Mr. Marigold's table, infinitely patient yet simultaneously brimming with anticipation. Its amber eyes, unchanged from its first iteration, constantly sought out its reflection in the silver mirror on the wall.

"No one has ever asked me how I wanted to look," the automaton confided, delicate fingers curling over Mr. Marigold's shoulder, their touch as light as a butterfly.

"Da Vinci's expertise was in art, not living creatures." An excuse, or perhaps an apology. "I'm no longer an it."

They stood, stretching, and their new shell stretched with them. It seemed they had stepped into the world fully formed, as natural as river water or a crane on the wing.

"Was that all you were to him?" Mr. Marigold asked.

"I was proof that he could create something intelligent."

Mr. Marigold nodded. He needed to ask, though he yearned for the answer and feared it in equal measure. "And what are you to me?"

The automaton's gaze was gentle and finally content. "I am proof that you will leave the world more beautiful than you found it."

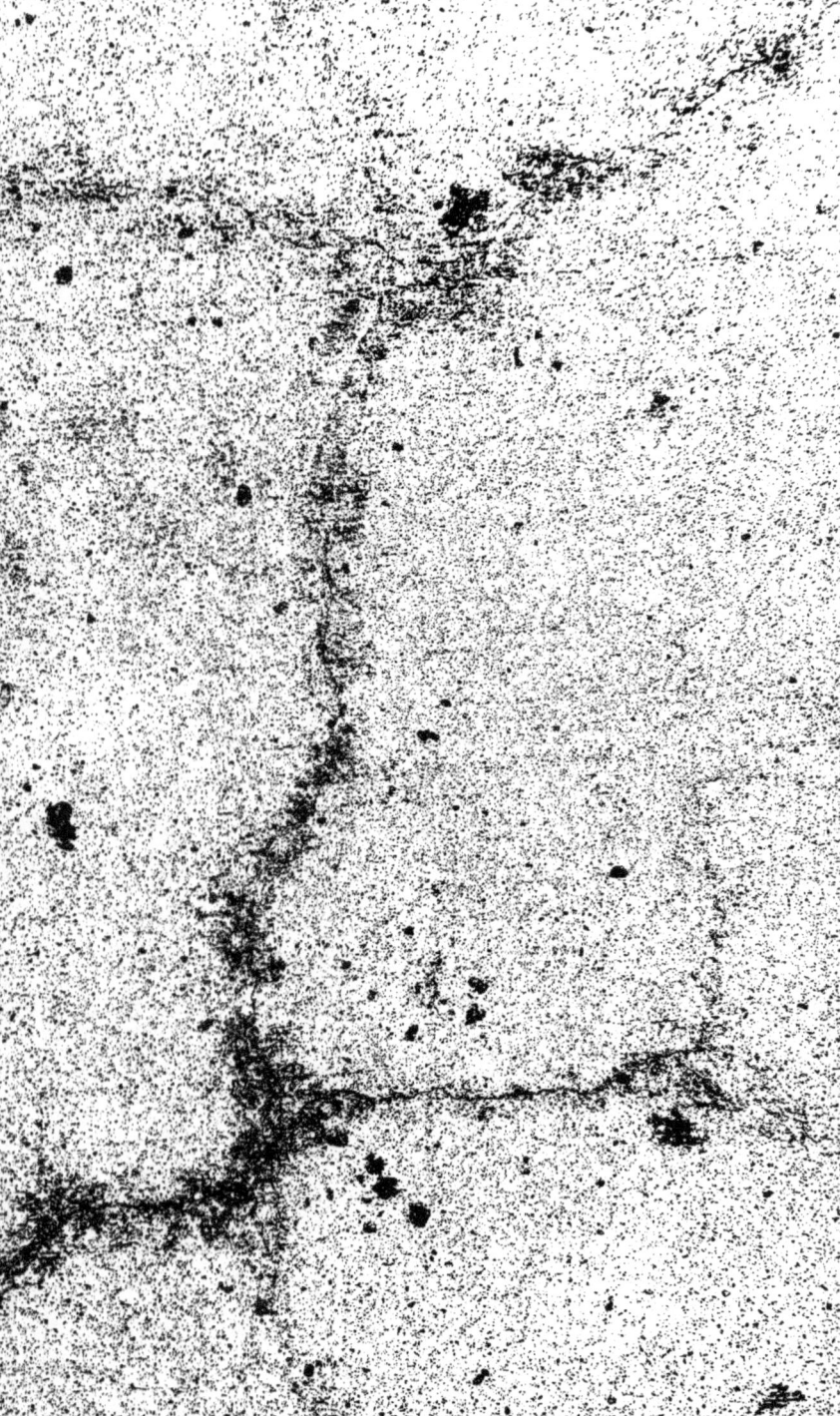

The Sigilist's Notes on the Fell Lord's Staff

Stephen Granade

ADDED SIGILS FOR fire blast, as the new adversary's armor reflects lightning.

Sanded off scorch marks.

At my lord's instruction, added leather for a more comfortable grip.

†

SANDED AWAY MORE scorch marks. My lord still uses lightning out of habit.

Sharpened the staff's top blades.

At my lord's instruction, adjusted the grip's location.

†

IMPROVED MIASMA SIGILS to increase range and efficacy.

Replaced the blade that snapped when fighting our adversary and their followers.

At my lord's instruction, will replace leather grip with "something that won't slip out of my hand, they nearly had my staff from me."

†

CARVED SIGILS INTO the leather grip to decrease slipperiness.
Didn't voice my worry about my lord's safety to him.

†

RE-SHARPENED THE BLADES.
Please let it be enough to protect him.

†

IT'S NOT THAT my lord would punish me. He forgives my
frailties.

My desires.

If I spoke unguardedly, I do not know what would spill
past my lips. Even the smallest crack in a dam is doomed
to widen.

So I confine my thoughts to these notes and hide them
where none can find them.

Must research a better sigil for the grip.

†

MY LORD HAS long enjoyed watching me ply my craft.
When he has time, he joins me in the castle basement. He
talks; I work on his staff until it becomes an extension of
his will made manifest by my art.

He tells me that our adversary has pressed their
advantage. My lord has lost some of the lands he had
seized, bringing order where before there was but chaos.

My lord will prevail. But he worries, and thus I worry.
The ache connects us, and I treasure it.

Also lengthened staff to improve reach.

†

ADDED NEW SIGILS. Anyone other than my lord or me who grasps it will be poisoned.

Let our adversary try to take the staff now.

†

TO SEE MY lord's face is to have your every inadequacy laid bare. The curve of his nose is an inevitability, his full lips an invitation. When I blink I see his visage, an afterimage carved like sigils.

With practice, I am able to look directly at him. It is a plunge in an icy lake, unbearable at first until I grow numb. Every time he returns to my workshop and removes his spiked helm, I must acclimate again.

Outside my workshop, he never removes that helm. I am glad, and not only because its sigils protect him. He is a language only I can read. I would not have anyone else learn it.

†

SO OUR ADVERSARY'S armor is now proof against fire? Let them try ice shards.

I labor over the sigils, working and re-working them into the staff's heartwood. Devotion wears a groove and, like all ritual, becomes its own reward.

†

I OVERHEARD THE castellan today remark to a courtier that I was "excessively loyal" to our lord.

He mistakes me. Are you loyal to your breath? It is a thing that you must have whether you want it or not.

†

OUR ADVERSARY'S ARMY surrounds our stronghold's walls.

They hold our river. Our water is lost.

My lord plans a quick strike, trusting his skill and mine to win the day.

I fear it will not work. Other enemies have shattered themselves against the granite of my lord's will. But not this adversary.

I have one last trick, a final, desperate gambit. I have successfully created sigils of teleportation.

Other sigilists have tried and failed. Hard enough to stretch a person, turn them needle-fine, and punch them through the world's skin. It is possible only if you use their true name to reshape them. Restoring them after is nearly impossible.

But not if you sacrifice an artifact of great power.

I tell him my plan. What it costs. What it requires: his true name.

He would be a fool to give it to me. Men such as him do not trust men such as me.

Without hesitation, he tells me.

With that name, I have all power over him. To remake him. To destroy him.

To save him.

The curve of the new sigils capture the essence of who he is. When I am done, I say, "Place your hands here and here." I slide them into position. My fingers are stubby, scarred embarrassments next to his long, supple ones. "Then will it, and you will be transported away from these lands."

"Leaving everyone behind."

"And this staff. It will snap, but you will be whole."

He falls silent. "Can your sigils carry more than one?"

His gaze heats the side of my face like a conflagration. I cannot look at him. "What do you mean, my lord?"

"Will they carry you as well?"

I do not answer.

He laces his fingers through mine. "Then I shall not use it."

I forget myself and turn to him. My eyes sting. "You

will. For me. For us." And then, "Hands here and here.'

His forehead is cool against my fevered brow. I do not recall how to breathe. "Hands here and here."

†

THE CRACK IS as unexpected and all-consuming as an earthquake. Stones tumble from the stronghold's towers.

Water trapped behind a dam turns stagnant. I should have remembered.

The castellan stands beside the adversary. He let them in without a fight.

The adversary squats beside where I am chained. "You abetted evil. But it is not too late. Make amends. Take me to him."

†

I SHAKE MY head but do not speak.

They drop the staff before me, broken like the castellan's vow. "You will take me to him."

Sanded away burn marks.

Re-carved sigils of power in the staff.

Attuned the staff to the adversary.

Banded the staff's center. It will not repair the crack. But it will hold. For a time.

†

MY LORD WAITS for me. I will return to him.

The adversary wishes to follow my lord? They would follow my lord through the world's skin? I alone can give that power to them. If they give me their true name.

And then I will destroy them.

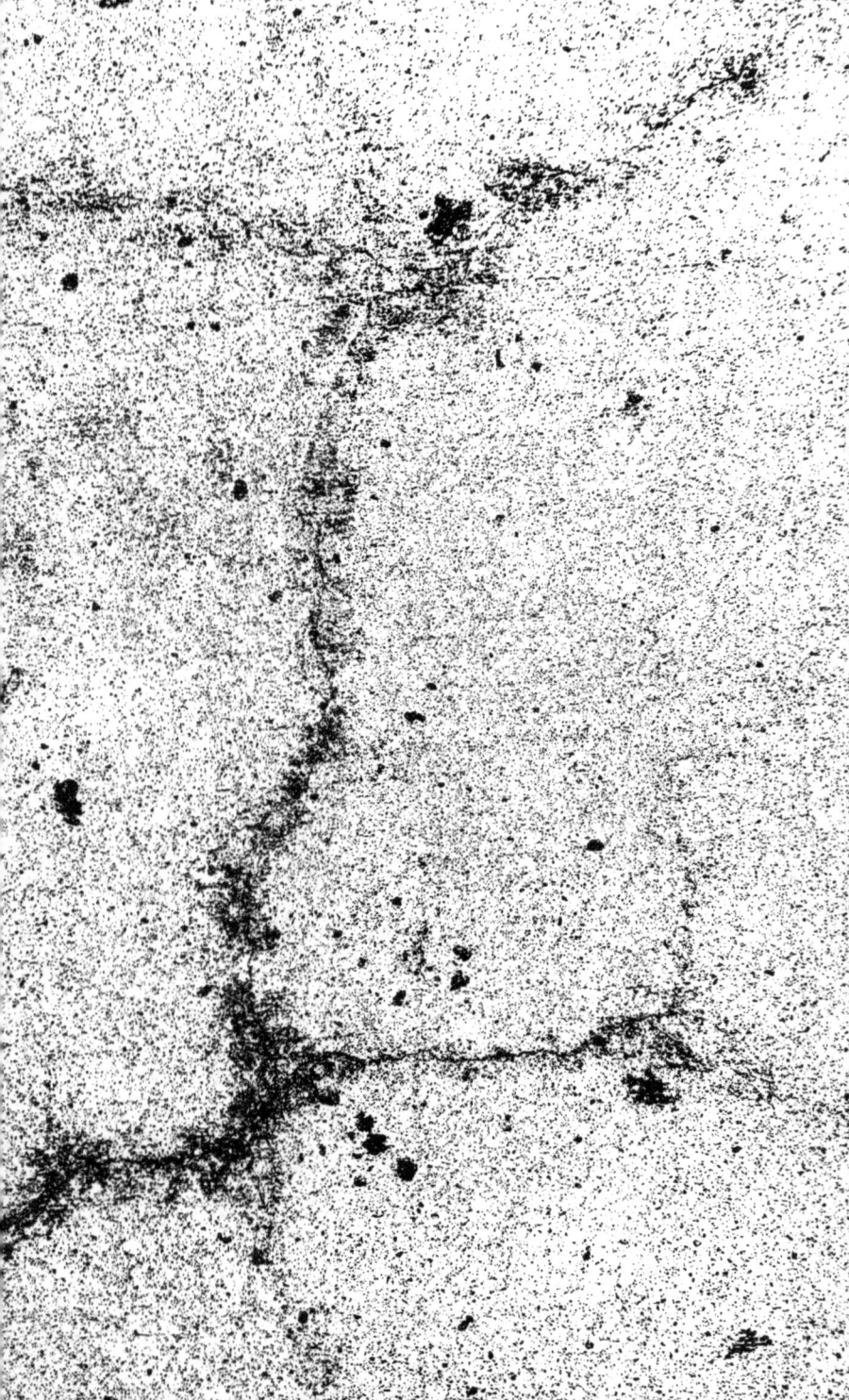

A Bridge Between

Miyuki Jane Pinckard

YOU'VE BEEN DEAD for three years. You were married to Takeshi and Irina, and my console chimes now with the notification that they're here to see you. My work crosses time zones; Kato's gentle snore from our bed on the other side of the room sounds melancholy. I clock in and pull on my rig.

I've studied your digital artifacts, your journals, films and photos, your social media presence. I've absorbed your quirks and the cadence of your speech. The algorithms can reproduce your voice and face, but the system needs a human actor to inhabit you.

Is it creepy? Yeah, a little. But the pay's too good to turn down.

I log into the virtual space my clients have chosen, a peaceful Japanese garden. You'd like it. You always loved plants and trees. It would remind you of the garden in Kyoto where you boldly proposed to Irina and Takeshi back when poly marriages still weren't legal. Irina stands on the bridge alone.

In your body, in your voice, I say, "It's good to see you."

She folds her arms around me. Around you. "I miss you."

She's wearing one of those expensive rigs that gives haptic feedback. She feels like she's really hugging you. I only get visual feedback, the fall of her hair as she moves in, the sweep of her cheek near mine. She releases you with a sigh.

Irina's eyes don't meet mine; she's agitated. I take her arm, and we walk slowly in the garden. Irina has chosen autumn, your favorite season. Golden leaves drift around us.

"Takeshi thinks we shouldn't see you anymore."

No surprise; he was reluctant from our first meeting to accept me as a substitute for you. "How do you feel about that?"

Irina gazes at the simulated bamboo grove in the distance. "I'm a coward. I never told you—"

My instinct tells me that she's close to expressing the reason she signed up for the service. In theory, we help our clients find closure. In practice, we're encouraged to draw out the process. "Tell me what?"

Irina's voice is raspy. "You don't smell like her. She had a scent, you know?"

That's the one thing we can't replicate. I don't know what you smelled like. That's a private memory I can't access. "What's bothering you?"

Her voice is so quiet. "Did you know I wasn't there?"

I've read the report. You had a stroke, alone, while Takeshi and Irina were away. They didn't find you until hours later and you died en route to the hospital. "It's not your fault, Irina."

"Then whose fault is it?" She turns away.

There are protocols for this, but I am you right now. . You confronted your mother's cancer when you were only twelve, you testified against your boss even though it got you fired. You always blazed through life. "Maybe it is. But what are you going to do about it now? I'm gone. *She's* gone."

Irina is silent, and I think she's crying although her rig doesn't convey tears.

I've broken about a hundred protocols and I know
they're monitoring this conversation. But you would hold
her hand and tell her the truth. "You won't find peace
talking to a dead woman."

She looks at you with startled eyes. At me.

I know what you would want, and it's the least I can
do, respect your wishes after I've embodied you. I let go of
Irina's hand. "This is goodbye. You shouldn't come back
here." Takeshi's right.

I watch as she crosses the bridge to the other side, until
she dissolves into the light. I know I won't see her again.

I take my headset off as my console chimes angrily
with notifications. My performance has been monitored,
evaluated. I shut it down. I peel myself out of my rig, get
a glass of water, and crawl under the covers next to Kato.
I press my nose into the back of their neck where the skin
is so soft. "I'll take the day off work tomorrow," I whisper.
"Let's go to the park, maybe. See some trees, smell the
air."

They sigh in their sleep and turn towards me.

Holding On

Ryan Breading

"I THINK I was a monster in a past life," Charlie says, apropos of nothing.

"And I was the queen of England," Drew answers dryly. "Want to see my crown? I've got it around here somewhere, it's *real* pretty."

They're lying on Drew's bed, looking up at the grey-brown stains on the ceiling as a forgettable tune plays on the radio. It's too hot to be outside right now—too hot to do anything, really, other than lie here in their underwear with the fan blowing stale air on their sweaty bodies. Drew misses the wintertime, when they could curl close to each other without it being unbearable.

"Ha ha," Charlie says. "I'm serious."

"How d'you know *I'm* not serious? I'd look great next to that gold piano."

"I keep having these weird dreams," Charlie continues, pointedly ignoring Drew. Fair enough. "Like I'm something else. Someone else. Sometimes I wake up and my limbs feel too long and I can taste blood on my teeth."

"Uncle Garrett would say that's because you don't floss," Drew remarks.

Charlie takes a swipe at them for that. Drew dodges him easily, but sees the shadows lingering in Charlie's eyes, the way he won't quite meet their gaze. That's not good. They take stock and decide the stifling heat is worth braving for this, rolling on top of Charlie and pinning his wrists playfully to the mattress, sparing a brief glance at Charlie's long, elegant fingers before they make eye contact.

"Listen to me. Everyone has strange dreams. It's just your subconscious being weird," Drew says, making their voice as reassuring as they can. "Human brains do that. It's normal, not some sign of being some kind of monster. Don't start torturing yourself, it doesn't help anyone."

Charlie sighs, his body finally relaxing under the weight of Drew's. "I know. Sorry."

"It's okay," Drew says. "I had a dream last night that freaked me out too."

"Yeah?"

"Yeah. I dreamt I was dating a complete idiot. Worst part is, I woke up and it was real."

"You *dork*," Charlie says, letting out a laugh.

"Your dork." Drew leans in obligingly when Charlie's fingers draw them close.

The kiss is too short for their liking but tasting that smile is worth *everything*, especially when they get to see the contentment on Charlie's face when they pull back. Then Charlie's kissing them again, oblivious to the rough scales appearing on his fingertips.

Drew would do anything for his beautiful face and its gap-toothed smile, their lips tingling from the kisses, and hopes to god that the spell will hold for just a little longer.

GASTRONOMIE MORTE

GERRI LEEN

THE RESTAURANT IS shuttered, the only illumination the light from the street—not that I need light. Vampires live in the shadows, darkness our natural home, and this place is familiar to me now.

I move through tables in a dining room no longer packed with customers. My stilettos click only because I spent a fortune on them and like to hear the sound. When I step into the kitchen, for a moment I pause and just...smell.

So many scents: a world of them colliding and transcending anything I could ever smell as a human. Food smells so good when you no longer need it

Blood, you see, has no taste—not to me now anyway. The copper tang I remember from licking a pricked finger when I was a human is gone. Pulsing in a neck, blood smells like heaven, but in the mouth, it becomes tasteless. Food is the same: it smells divine but even dunked in blood, it only adds texture, not flavor.

I'm pragmatic enough to settle in for what I can still experience, opening the refrigerators, sniffing this or that container, letting the scent of a fresh strawberry transport me to a time when I wasn't this way.

Too long ago.

Not long at all.

Not so long ago that I can't still mourn the loss of things like brunch and cookouts during the day. But too long to remember how champagne bubbles taste when they flitter across the tongue, how painful an ice-cream headache could be, or the sated drowsiness of a post holiday meal.

I hear footsteps only seconds before someone calls out, "Who's there?"

The chef who lives upstairs is back. I've let myself become so lost in scents and memories that I didn't hear her come in, didn't smell her blood over the other aromas.

I slip into the shadows as she moves deeper into the kitchen.

She seems more curious than afraid. "You've been here before. I've smelled your perfume."

It's another thing I pay a fortune for so it's not a common one.

"I can make you food—if you're hungry." She sounds... lonely as she flips on a light that illuminates one of the cooktops.

I've watched this place many times after the sun goes down. It's nothing but chaos during the dinner hour, and she's always at the center of it. How can she sound so alone?

I move so I can see her better, but I'm still shrouded in shadow. "I like the smell of your food, but I'm not hungry."

Technically accurate, but oh what I'd give for one true taste.

She looks around but of course doesn't find me—she'll wait forever if she's trying to hear me breathe or move. Finally, she whispers into the silence, "How did you get in?"

"Picked the lock." Which is true. Breaking windows is for amateurs. Besides, I want to be able to come back.

"All to smell my food?"

I decide to give her a version of the truth. "I can smell but not taste."

"Normally it's smell that's crucial to taste."

"What can I say?"

I should leave, should come back some other day and not let my stilettos snap in the same way she snaps her knives when she chops and minces—did I want her to find me?

But before I can flee, she pulls out a pan. "What are your favorite dishes?"

I want to tell her: halibut cheeks in butter and lime; chicken simmering in pineapple and chilies; lamb, savory with cumin and coriander. But to what end?

"Sit," she says and I finally come into the light.

For a moment she stops at the sight of me. I am beautiful but also so pale—the color of egg whites or mushroom flesh or a lacy meringue.

I can tell she knows what I am. And we stand, waiting, until she says, "Did you come to kill me?" She even reaches for a wooden spoon, and I laugh because it's so charmingly brave.

"No, I really did just come to smell the food." I sit on a stool, near enough that she can study me more easily, but not so close I'll unnerve her more than I already have.

She's clearly unsure, but then she puts the spoon down and smiles. "So...nothing with garlic then?" Before I can answer, she says: "Food allergies are a bitch."

"I miss garlic," I say as she begins to chop.

"I bet you do. It's delicious. But there's a world of flavors out there." She passes me a bowl of a crumbled tan spice and asks me to guess what it is.

I smell savory and citrus, and she seems delighted when I say that. She also enjoys that I fail to identify it as ground dried lime and explains with passion why and how she uses it.

She holds out another bowl and when I fail again, her smile grows.

The evening passes, as she cooks and I move from the stool to stand beside her, looming over the pans, inhaling the aromas of the dishes she makes and then sets aside to cool. Until I feel the dawn approaching.

"I have to go. Thank you for this."

She eyes all the things she's made for me. She hasn't tasted—perhaps out of some form of solidarity.

"A waste," I whisper.

"I'll taste them once you're gone—see if any are good enough to end up on the menu."

I turn away but before I can get to the door, she asks, "Same time tomorrow?"

That would be a mistake. My life requires me to remain unknown and unknowable.

And yet I turn to her. "Yes, tomorrow."

"Any requests?"

I smile in a way that I haven't for a very long time. "Surprise me."

Illusions of Freedom

Oluwatomiwa Ajeigbe

1.

TONIGHT, WE ARE birds. Folarin has chosen the form of a nightjar while I have gone with my favorite form, that of a barn owl. Tonight, we spread our wings and tour the night sky. We fly above the clouds, to a place beyond judgement and hatred. Tonight, we are free.

2.

BY DAY, WE are prisoners of self. We are conscious of the watching eyes and pointing fingers. There is too much attention on us. We cannot take off the human flesh that drags us down and whisper our tired selves into the form of a free creature. By day, we are not free.

3.

IT IS A terrible thing to be marked by the eyes of the world.

It is known, in this village, that witches are the only ones capable of changing their shape and there is a standing rule concerning witches: they are burnt at the stake.

Folarin and I were careless one night. We slipped back into our human forms while a hunter watched. He alerted everyone in the village. Since then, suspicious eyes have followed us everywhere. They want to see us slip into another form, to confirm what the hunter said. So we have been more careful. To confirm what they have heard would be as good as signing our own death warrants.

There are many who believe that the lifeblood of those like us possesses magical qualities. These people watch and hound us as well, waiting for us to let our guard down, so they might creep up on us in the dark, a sharp knife ready to reap our souls.

Thus far, we have evaded them. We are still free.

4.

THE SECOND REASON why we are watched is because we have found love in the most unlikely of places. Our love is frowned upon by the people of this cruel world. Our love is called an abomination. They watch us, grinding their teeth, waiting for the day they can feed our bodies to the fire.

These people—our people—believe in the cleansing power of fire. They burn haunted houses, rapists, witches and abominations. In their eyes, what I share with Folarin is a stain on their collective white garment that can only be washed away by the flames.

Two girls were once caught making love by the river bank. They were marched into the village by the people and pelted with rotting fruits. The hearing was brief. The judgement was predictable: death by burning.

A priestess from the cult of Oshun, the goddess of purity, presided over the burning. I was there with Folarin. He wouldn't look at me; we had argued on the way. He wanted us to change shape and save the girls somehow but I refused. Folarin was younger than I am and rarely thought of consequences.

The priestess said a prayer of cleansing and made a motion with her hand. There was a collective intake of breath from the onlookers as the terrified girls were set on fire. I shut my eyes but their agonized screams pierced my heart. Folarin's hand found mine and I squeezed it reassuringly.

That night, we ran into the fields and chose the form of snakes. I became a king cobra that night and Folarin was a brooding viper. He turned his cold reptilian eyes to me sometime during the night and spoke in his hissing voice and I could hear the worry in his voice.

"Tolu, promise me we won't end up like that. Promise me."

I looked at him, at the love of my life, curled up and anxious in a barren field under the night sky. I couldn't give a reassuring smile as a snake so I just touched my mouth to his.

"I promise, my love." I hissed. "Someday, we will leave and never return. Someday, we will be free."

5.

WE KNOW HOW this will end. It is like a play we have seen too many times. There is no plot twist that can take us by surprise.

The both of us have made our decisions. Folarin has chosen me and I have chosen survival. I will do whatever it takes to keep us safe. Tonight, we are free. We are birds, singing of freedom from the sky. We will shed our wings and feathers and slip back into our bodies before the sunrise. We will kiss each other goodbye and go home. We will endure the stares and whispers and pointing fingers. And at night, we will meet again and decide on which form to take.

We will do this over and over. And maybe one day the knife that walks through the dark will find our hearts. But before that happens, we will witness these semblances of freedom each night, as long as we can.

Before we die, we will live.

ELASTIC COLLISIONS

TJ BERRY

ONE MIGHT ASSUME that Arthur is my teacher, because of his advanced age and my relative youth, but we are nothing of the sort. One might guess we are brothers, because of the similar bulge in the tips of our noses, but that is also untrue. He is not my father, nor I his child. Arthur and I are colleagues, collaborators, conspirators, and consorts.

Our fingers dance in practiced rhythm across a great machine. We move gears and press levers, careful not to become tangled in the vicious spinning works. The machine is more ancient than the stars and has also not been inverted yet.

Arthur and I have always worked in tandem. His deliberate motions emerge from wisdom while my agile choices spring from the plasticity of youth. We operate in constant tension. I sigh heavily and hasten his languid stratagems. He *tsks* out loud and overrules my sweeping changes. Together, we tweak the lines of time, moving seats of power, saving future leaders from childhood accidents, and sacrificing villages to save nations.

In the rare instances when the timelines are quiet—
after treaties have been signed and bellies are full—we
steal an intimate moment to ourselves. Arthur's slightest
touch can ignite a fire within me. He knows all the
pressure points that cause my brain to short circuit. He
anticipates my every desire. I never have to ask.

The machine pings a despot's initial rise to power, but
we linger for one last moment in each other's arms. Lying
in the dark, dizzy and slick, my thumb grazes the stub of
Arthur's torn ear. The edge is a ragged half-circle that
looks as if it's been bitten off by a ravenous creature.

"Time to work," he whispers into my collarbone.

I'm more exhausted than before our respite, but
Arthur's eyes twinkle with the energy of youth. It hasn't
escaped my notice that he seems younger all the time.
His skin feels more tumescent beneath my fingers and
his breath comes faster and less laboriously each time we
make love.

Back at the machine, I tweak the timeline to undo
a global pandemic and save a million lives. Arthur
pretends not to notice my flirting. When he executes a
deft merger between three alternate realities, resulting in
the accidental death of a fascist ruler before he comes to
power, I know he's showing off for me. I lean forward to
tell him so and the machine grabs at my robe, drawing
my head into its spinning jaws.

Two unstoppable gears catch my right ear between
them. Their teeth mash together, tearing away cartilage
and lobe. Arthur's face crumples in agony. He yanks me
back. I drip blood into the works, setting off a barbarous
genocide. I can barely draw a breath through the blinding
pain. Arthur cradles my head, allowing pestilence to
claim ten thousand while he presses a bandage to my ear.
I clutch the side of my head, dizzy and slick.

"You could have warned me," I gasp.

"You never do," he replies.

There are no mirrors in this place, so I peel away the bandage and run my thumb along the sticky wound. The gears have bitten out a ragged semi-circle. Arthur watches my widening eyes with patient amusement.

"We're the same," I say.

"We are," says Arthur. "We have always been and always will be. One moving forward, one moving back. So it was and so it will be infinitely."

I reach out with bloody fingers and spin the gears with a ferocity that escalates a tense standoff into a Great War. Arthur reaches past me and gently undoes the damage.

"Is our labor a punishment?" I ask.

Arthur laughs loudly and the gears wobble on their axes... the genocide ends, a cure for the pestilence is discovered, and ten thousand babies are conceived. "You'll see," he says, pressing his cool lips to my burning temple.

POD 530217-A

EMMA LINDHAGEN

ON THURSDAY, I am killing Mx. Clark.

Officially, I'm discontinuing account no. 530217 and overseeing the disposal of the contents of pod 530217-A, the only pod associated with the aforementioned account. I am signing the papers required to execute the discontinuation, transporting the contents to the incinerator in the basement of Cryonics Inc. and then delivering the urn to the disposal station. I am doing this because the payee of account no. 530217, namely the descendant of Mx. Clark, has elected not to extend the subscription of account no. 530217 for the preservation of the contents of pod 530217-A, namely Mx. Clark, and has also elected not to receive the remains for interment.

Unofficially, I am killing Mx. Clark, a 51-year-old legal secretary with a family history of cancer who consented to have themself placed in cryopreservation because they genuinely believed that someday they would wake up in a world where cancer no longer exists. I am doing it because their great-great-grandchild, an ill-payed food service worker, has at last become unable to afford keeping their ancestor in what I have firmly come to believe is nothing more than a glorified freezer.

In the file associated with the pod, it says that Mx.
Clark's favorite dish is pork schnitzel with sparkling
rosé, and that they enjoy bossa-nova. That is really all it
says.

As a child, I spent countless hours among the rows
of pods. I would pick a playmate from among them
and sit next to them, telling stories. I can't remember
anymore if I actually believed they could hear me or if
I just wanted company when my parents were working
and my siblings were too adolescent to play with me.
I read their files, once I learned to read, so I could
speak to them about the things they cared about. The
files taught me about classical music, about early 21st
century soap operas, about astronomy. Every month
there was a new activity. I begged my parents to let
me try snowboarding, crochet, juggling, parkour,
programming, stamp collecting...

At night, lying in bed in our apartment at the top
floor of the facility, waiting for sleep to settle over my
mind, I saw them before my inner eye, waking up and
rising from their pods, reunited with their families
decades or centuries after death. That part of it, I know
I believed.

At school, I was "Freezer-kid". I didn't mind, not
really. The taunts didn't bite as much as the loneliness
did. My best friend Kara wasn't allowed to visit me
at home. When we were thirteen, she came to visit
anyway, and I snuck her down into the storage rooms.
She stood amid all the pods, among all my childhood
friends, and cried. She never asked to visit after that. It
was around then that my heart slowly started breaking.

By then, I suspect my parents' hearts had already
broken clean in half. Cryonics Inc. has been a family
business for over a hundred years. Once, it stood at the
forefront of an industry which brought hope in a time

when it was sorely needed, but that hope has dwindled as new technologies have risen up to overshadow it. Cloning, android avatars that allow people to leave their physical body safely at home, brain-uploads— these have all chipped away at the legacy that Cryonics Inc. was supposed to be for me and my siblings, for my hypothetical children.

Last year, someone learned how to upload a consciousness not into a cloud or an android, but into a VR-space. Debate still rages about whether existing only in VR can really be called living, but nevertheless clients flock to the technology.

But it isn't the competing technologies that are slowly ruining us, not really. My ancestors loaded their fortune onto a sinking ship, it just took a few generations until this was evident. The crass truth is that the science just isn't there. Even after all these years, we haven't found a safe way to revive those frozen in cryonic sleep.

When I was little, my parents would offer clients whose pod subscriptions had expired—and whose families had not claimed their bodies—to researchers experimenting with new methods of revival. I still remember how the phone would ring, how my mother would say into the receiver that she understood. How quiet the house got for a day or two every time it just didn't work. Eventually, the requests for test subjects stopped coming. The scientific community agreed that revival simply wasn't possible. Since then, the pods have been emptying slowly, one-by-one. No new clients have signed up in over fifteen years. My siblings never came back from college, and my parents have long since moved, leaving me in charge. My father wrings his hands over the phone, lamenting the future he didn't manage to give me.

The first time I executed a cancellation on my own, I cried all the way from the incinerator to the disposal unit, tears spilling onto the urn. The second time, I turned to the biography file instead, deciding that a stranger's joy was a better send-off than a stranger's tears. That night, I had penne ala arabiata for the first time and tried my hand at macrame in honor of a retired history teacher who'd suffered a traumatic heart attack. This became my custom—enjoy their life to mark their death.

On Thursday, I am killing Mx. Clark. Once the urn containing their remains has been disposed of, I will go back to my apartment at the top floor of the facility. There, a bottle of sparkling rosé will be waiting for me in the refrigerator together with a ready-to-fry pork schnitzel, potato wedges, and peas. I'll play bossa-nova on the old record player I bought last summer at a yard sale.

I won't cry for Mx. Clark while I have their last meal, or while I lay on the sofa and let the music and the alcohol fill my senses.

I'll cry for Mx. Clark when I go to bed that night, pull the covers up to my chin, and remember those nights long ago when I believed with my whole unbroken heart that one day they would come back to life.

The Little Time We Have

Georgia Cook

A T 1PM, THEIR apartment was cocooned in darkness. The curtains were drawn, letting only the thinnest stands of sunlight through the cracks. All was calm. All was still.

One of Olivia's arms was flung over the duvet, the other around Katie.

Katie listened to her own heartbeat, wondering if the pigeons had huddled on the pavement outside again. Olivia's arm was cold against her chest; Olivia's arm was always cold.

Slowly, slowly, Katie extracted herself, shuffled to the edge of the bed, and stood, stifling first a yawn, then a shiver. Olivia had turned the heating on last night, but the air remained sharp with a subterranean chill.

†

KATIE OFTEN THOUGHT it was the little quirks in a relationship that stood out. Olivia's apartment, for a start: the basement floor of a Victorian townhouse, hemmed on all sides by high converted warehouses and office blocks. Almost no natural light, almost no natural anything, and always an abundance of rats.

Olivia was fond of rats.

†

KATIE FUMBLED HER way to the kitchen, retracing yesterday's path through the maze of furniture and old books. Their clothes lay scattered on Olivia's antique rug; Olivia's underwear hung carelessly off the dresser in the corner, entwined with Katie's tights.

With care, Katie could almost—*almost*—find her way around the flat without turning on the lights. Olivia had laughed when Katie tried to demonstrate this one night, and asked why on earth she'd try.

Katie suspected the lights in the flat were maintained purely for her sake—that Olivia spent her free time ambling around in the pitch black, and had adopted bulbs purely as a relationship compromise.

†

THEN THERE WAS the kitchen.

Olivia kept a kitchen in the same way other people kept exercise equipment: with the vague notion of maybe using it some day, on a whim, if she was bored. Everything in here with a practical purpose was Katie's. The kettle. The mugs (the cracked pink kitten mug she'd placed proudly in the cupboard after their fifth date; the Dracula mug that had sent Olivia into hysterics on Valentine's day.) The large jar of instant coffee on the top shelf, hers.

Katie reached up on her tiptoes and took down the jar, spooning it into two mugs. While she waited for the kettle to boil, she eased herself up onto the counter and sat, legs dangling, trying to rub some life back into her arms.

Upstairs, she could hear the gentle thuds of the retired schoolteacher in the first floor flat. Mrs. Cabler referred to Katie as "Sweetheart" and Olivia as "That Dear Old Thing." Katie had glanced through Mrs. Cabler's door once, and seen a living room furnished in glistening monochrome photographs and knitted furniture covers. She wondered how long Olivia and Mrs Cabler had known one another. Sometimes Katie wondered—in those long, deep afternoons while Olivia slept—if Olivia would still know her when she too was old and grey. Perhaps she would also one day live alone above Olivia's flat, watching the tides of lovers pass through the basement door, while Olivia remained as she always had: eternally herself.

How much time did they have left until then? Had Olivia done this all before? How much time would be enough to make their relationship...real?

†

THE SUNFLOWERS WERE Olivia's, sitting in their vase on the kitchen table, bought fresh from the florist on the corner. Olivia had smiles through the stems, watching as Katie ate her takeaway pizza, then made tea for herself in the glowing sunset.

Food was an aesthetic experience for Olivia: she liked steaming cups of coffee and neatly arranged charcuterie boards, crisp red apples and pungent cheeses. She loved tiny cafes with vintage cutlery, and the joy of letting a croissant go cold in front of her.

Beauty, she'd called it once. *Normal* beauty. Tiny moments stretched into long ones. Life made to last.

"Take me for afternoon tea," she'd insisted on their

second date. "Invite me to barbecues. Let me meet your parents. It's been two hundred years of bloody *atmosphere*, this time around I want something *nice*."

†

THAT WAS KATIE's compromise, at least as far as Oivia was concerned. No midnight meetings on rain drenched rooftops; no stolen kisses in shadowy nightclubs. No mystique, no menace. And absolutely no Gothic churches.

Just niceness. Just *normality*. The era of flashing fangs and lacy corsets was over and done with.

†

...BARRING THE OCCASIONAL bit of roleplay, of course.

†

KATIE WOUND THROUGH the darkness back to the bedroom, coffee mugs balanced in both hands. Olivia had propped herself up amongst the pillows, watching the world through half-slitted eyes.

"Nobody, my love," she said, as Katie eased herself carefully back into bed. "makes a cup of coffee quite as *loudly* as you."

Olivia rested her ear against Katie's chest, her hair fanning across Katie's nightclothes , blonder than blonde. Tousled from sleep.

"What are you *doing*?" Katie exclaimed. "You'll spill the coffee, look!"

"I like to listen," mumbled Olivia. "It sounds nice."

Katie batted her away with a laugh. "Yeah, *well*, your ear's bloody cold!"

Olivia took a coffee mug from Katie and pressed it

to her ear. The steam twisted up towards the ceiling, ghostlike in the warm dark of the bedroom. Olivia pulled the mug away, then leaned in with a grin.

"Better?" she asked.

†

KISSING OLIVIA WAS strange; colder and sharper than any kiss she'd ever experienced. She'd cut Katie's lip, that first tentative date so many months ago, and in the December chill had cradled Katie's chin in her hands, whispering soft apologies. Katie hadn't minded. Katie never minded.

†

OLIVIA SETTLED BACK down amongst the pillows on her side of the bed, winding her fingers through Katie's hair. Her fingers were just as cold as her arm, just as cold as her kiss.

"I want to stay like this," she mumbled. "Just you and me, here beneath the world. Tucked in bed forever. It's so perfect. So utterly perfect."

Slowly, slowly, Olivia stilled. She wouldn't move again until evening.

†

KATIE LAY IN the gloom, thinking about tonight, when they could finally open the curtains and step outside. They'd walk the streets, or go to a 24 hour cafe. She thought about the night after that, and the night after that: all the nights they would spend together, all of them finite. All of them *theirs*. She thought of right now: a halfway point between living and waiting.

She thought of every lover before her; every lover Olivia would take after she was gone. Every spark of adoration. She thought of the flowers in the kitchen, the giggling afternoon teas, the walks in the rain,

Every second a glittering soap bubble, fractured and fragile. Olivia cradled each one, stretched them into infinity. Stamped them across the world like pinned butterflies. Like tiny jewels.

Love held gently, no matter how fleeting.

Love made to last.

BRIGHTER THAN STARS

PRERY RUHLAND

I.

A COMET TORE through the sky when the Boy-Emperor was born. "That will be you one day," his mother told him. "Brighter than stars."

II.

UPON ASCENSION TO the high throne, the Boy-Emperor decreed that no subject from the Atlantic to the Nile would be permitted to keep their face. For faces, the Boy-Emperor declared, held the essence of beauty, and beauty was treacherous in the manner of politicians and land-owners. Only the Boy-Emperor, with a face like the sun, and spring, and a thousand blooming orchids, could be trusted to wield such a deadly weapon.

And so it was, in the first days of his reign, that cumbersome stone masks were distributed among the populace. They were the most grotesque complexions imaginable.

III.

THE BOY-EMPEROR'S DECREE was enforced with utmost impunity, and within the first year of his reign, not a single subject—be they slave or senator—ever removed their terrible masks. When the Boy-Emperor addressed his people, he addressed crowds of drooling cyclopes, hissing gorgons, and fork-tongued satyrs, and in turn, they saw the sole example of human beauty the land had left to offer. He was their light, their God, and oh how he cherished it.

The Boy-Emperor's rule was defined by his pleasures. He held lavish banquets amongst masked aristocrats, he oversaw bloody duels between masked gladiators, and at the end of every day, he would retire to his bedchambers, beckon forth his harem of the most virile men of the empire, and engage in one great, masked orgy.

IV.

IT WAS AT one such orgy that the Boy-Emperor's decadent reign came to an end. He was naked save for his onyx crown, his rectum filled by a beaked harpy's length and his lips pursed around the dripping head of a grinning ghoul. The Boy-Emperor had drunk more than usual, and decided that this man before him, with his puckered prick and sculpted arse, might be the finest specimen he had ever bedded. So, swallowing the ghoul's ejaculate and shoving the harpy away, the Boy-Emperor vowed at once that he would break his sacred rule—he would unmask this handsome stranger, and the Boy-Emperor would be his bride.

Giggling, the Boy-Emperor reached below the ghoul's chin to exhume his true face. Yet, to the Boy-Emperor's horror, he felt only flesh, and the ghoul's grin widened, for his mask was no mask at all. The Boy-Emperor yelped and fell back, back into the arms of the harpy, of the cyclops, of the satyr, of the gorgon, of the hungry things with gnashing jaws and buzzing cocks, of the beasts of his own design.

V.

WHEN THE SERVANTS entered the Boy-Emperor's chambers, they beheld no beasts, no lovers, no festivities. All they saw was their regent tangled in satin sheets, his eyes frozen in abject terror, a dribble of crimson glistening from his lips. In the days to come, the people would shed their masks. They would tear down his statues, they would free their cities, they would reach forth to greet a new dawn.

In the outer reaches of space, a great cluster of frozen debris dissolved in a polychromic flame. But for a moment, the Boy-Emperor burned brighter than stars.

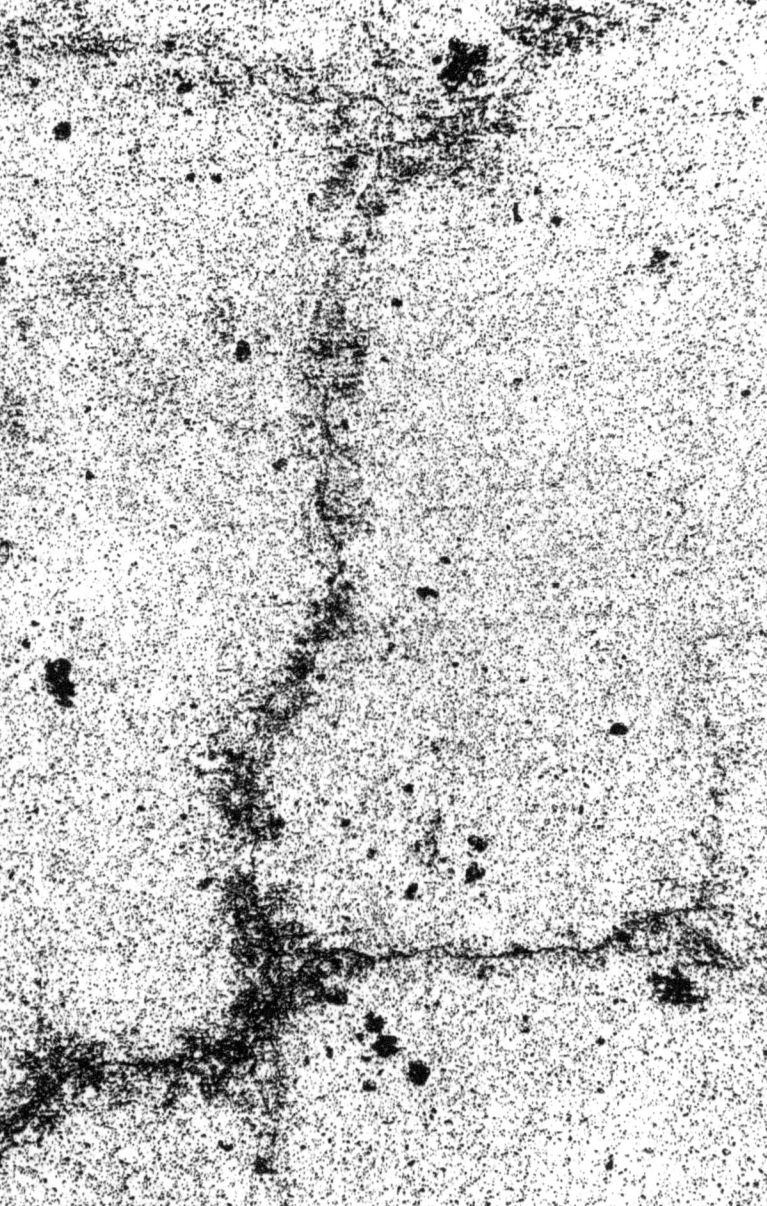

VERY FAST AND VERY FAR APART

AJ LUCY

THE GUY WHO tested the human body's limits during violent deceleration was named John Stapp, and Jody still thinks that's funny. Stapp the stopping man.

Her name's Jody Hart, and that's funny in the other direction, because she's never cared a lot about anyone.

A hard stop facing forward during deceleration causes "red outs" as the blood pushes up against your retinas and busts through your capillaries. Face backwards, get "white outs;" the blood vacates your eyes and sets up residence in the back of your skull.

It's safer to hit the ground with your back to it.

†

"I'M DELILAH BELL, I'll be your radio and mission contact for the next tour."

"Jody Hart."

"Our apogee is every five and a half hours, and so that's when we'll call you."

"I take it we'll be seeing a lot of each other, then."

"Technically not *seeing*, ma'am."

"Then I'll be hearing you, Delilah Bell."

†

IN SPACE, YOU conserve two things: fuel and momentum.

In the aviation age, long-range flights would be refueled by big fuel tanker planes with a robotic boom. The two aircraft match speed until, to each other, they are still. To the ground, they're hurtling along at six hundred miles an hour. They hang in the illusion of stillness granted by their reference frame, two pilots tied by a radio and a boom-mounted camera, two planes linked like dragonflies mating, until the tank is full.

These days, it's easy to intercept a refuel and rations module: she goes on the comms and says, hey crew, we're catching some R&R tonight, gonna stay in and watch video-on-demand with our honeys, gonna make sure the coupler slips right into the receiver collar, if you know what I mean, and I mean it literally, because if we miss this docking we'll all starve to death in space.

It's not easy, because they're clocking six hundred miles per second, but it's easier, because on the fuel intercept everybody cooperates.

†

"WHAT'S OUR NEXT target, Radio-Girl?"

"Civilian communication satellites, ma'am."

"It's about to get real lonely out there for a whole lotta people."

"But you don't get lonely."

"Nope."

†

IN A STALEMATE, violence gets put off as long as everybody stays afraid. The feds have Jody up in space as a big Beware Of Dog sign, taking potshots every six months to show off how good they are at hitting tiny things from a long way off.

You get a couple hour-long windows once every couple months and then it's waiting until the orbits align again. Distances get big fast, and their reflexes are limited by the speed of their messages. In this cold war, even light is slow.

†

"SO, WHAT DO you look like?"

"Like ground beef with a buzz cut."

"I bet you're fearsome in full dress."

"I can make a non-qual shit his pants from fifty feet away."

"I like that."

†

THEY GO FULL dark after every strike. It's the most dangerous part of every mission, when the other side gets hard data on where they are: missile trajectories mean reverse-engineered orbital calculations.

Nobody's even allowed to vent the lav, because all that released pressure causes vibrations.

In one of the earliest space missions, a leaking urine bag caused an electrical short that almost killed them. Jody tells the crew, and everyone laughs and double-checks their valves.

So far, nobody is trying to hit crewed spacecraft. It's not any more challenging than hitting satellites, but it's an escalation the Jupiter-based secessionists don't want to make yet.

†

"YOU SHOULD CALL me Jo."

"We aren't supposed to use the channel for this, you know."

"I won't tell if you don't."

"You'd be the officer I'd be obligated to tell, Jo."

"Then it's not a problem."

†

WHEN SHE WAS thirty-four, Jody had to make the decision to take her mom off a ventilator. It was a bad death—DNR is the way to go, in documents and in the RFID chip in your dog tags.

Jody treated it like any other task that had to be done.

She signs off on their first crewed target and it feels the same. Their goal is picked for them, a big hulking piece of space infrastructure. It's a soft mark, too massive to re-direct without burning more fuel than the tanker has to spare.

She leads her crew through it, a series of jobs to be done carefully, just like sharpshooting, or paperwork, or holding her mother's hand.

†

"SOMEONE'S GOING TO try to hit you back. I'm not stupid, Jo. I can look at our missions and guess the other guys are doing the same, and you're an attractive kill."

"Don't think about that."

"I'll think what I want."

"I'm getting old. Soon I'll be out of this tin can. I'll buy you a house in New Mexico. Somewhere with a big outside. Just for us, Dee."

"Not if you die first."

"Haven't died yet, don't plan to later. Promise."

"You ought to be shit-scared of leaving me alone down here."

"Guess I'm out of practice."

†

IT'S NOT JODY'S fault that her team's the best at what they do. Her numbers girl has a knack for estimation, better than the inflexible computer model can come up with, and her guy on the ship's sensor-based eyes is uncanny at picking signal out of noise. She can sometimes hear him listening to static off-shift.

The easy metaphors don't work in orbit. You think of it like naval warfare, or billiards, because it's hard to imagine so much free-wheeling three-dimensional space. Everything on a planet has a relationship with earth and sky.

†

"DELILAH, COME IN."

†

"DELILAH."

†

"DEE."

†

"BABY, PLEASE."

"C'MON, HONEY. Everybody dies someday."

WHAT GETS THEM is an electromagnetic pulse, 400 miles across, the cheater's way to aim. It hits every circuit board on the ship like a fist to the chin and has the crew diving for oxygen masks and the manual pressure cranks. There's always a mask less than fifteen seconds away. No more complaining about drills, Jody says. Drills are why you lot are pros, sucking plastic like kids snorkeling on the beach, picking up bits of busted beer bottles and calling them sea glass.

Command sends up a shuttle with spare parts and a pack of computer engineers. They perform the coupling blind, cameras dead, eyes clouded by fogging oxygen masks.

Over the radio, Jody can hear the pilot on the shuttle holding his breath. He'll have a partner in his ear too: don't drift, man, gently, gently, overshoot and you've killed them.

"COMMANDER HART, THIS is mission control. How do you read?"

"It's okay, Dee. We're never gonna hit the ground."

To Exhale Sky

Shingai Njeri Kagunda

KILA HAS ALWAYS been able to turn grief into tiny little things.

When Dimples, the family dog, dies at age five, Kila pulls all the sadness inside her and breathes out a cowrie shell. A small greyish cowrie shell that shimmers when the sun shines on it from a certain angle. Her grandmother makes her a necklace while singing a song about how the cowrie shell—such a small thing—became the totem of her tribe—such a big tribe. Every time Kila breathes something new, her grandmother sings a different version of this song.

Years later, after getting off her stage at Kencom, Kila runs into a man in a deserted alley near Kenyatta Avenue. He has a gun and tells her to run, but only after she gives him all her money. It is just after 6pm and the Nairobi sun is starting to set, the darkness taking over the space the light has left.

The man grabs the shell necklace Kila's grandmother had made for Kila. "Please no, tafadhali I beg."

The man hits her. "Shut up!"

Kila holds her purse up, her eyes squeezed shut. The man

freezes when Kila opens her mouth and screams out stars. Two bright balls of fire the size of pupils float out into the air between them. He drops the necklace and runs away, blinded by their light, but they follow, penetrating his skin, burning into his core. Kila places the necklace back around her neck and takes a shaky breath in.

A few years after this, Kila falls in love with Tam, who she first saw on a Tuesday morning grabbing a coffee across the room at the Java on Mama Ngina street before work. Tam makes her inhale big, beautiful things into herself. Brown eyes, slightly slanted, small, locked dreads, dimples that accompany a smile, and two nose piercings, one on each nostril.

All small things attached to this big love which tumbles and unfurls over a glance, two numbers exchanged, first coffee date where dawa is spilled onto white pants with yellow daisies, hand grabbed to prevent a tragic death by accident on the of course crazy busy streets of Nairobi—laughter—so much laughter about everything and anything and nothing, and bathroom kisses in restaurants between whispered secrets of big love.

When Kila dreams of Tam and their secret big love that carries pasts and presents into the spaces between them, she feels herself inhale buildings, taste cities, and swallow continents. With Tam, Kila forgets what—if anything—is big and what is small.

Tam loves looking up at the sky, pays attention to the clouds, constantly contemplates the sun, and sighs at the moon and stars. Maddening as a wordless poet.

"Tell me," Kila teases her love, gulping down the picture of Tam's eyes. Tam is the shape of the world within Kila.

"Everything looks so small from down here," Tam says, "so far away. While up there, it is this whole expanse. Yani, we can't even imagine how large and fierce those balls of

fire are." She kisses Kila's neck softly. "And in our little
humanness, we have the audacity to sing, *twinkle twinkle little
star.*"

Kila touches the cowrie shell attached to the necklace
on her heart. That night she dreams of swallowing the
sky. The little big thing for her little big love.

Cancer is the thing that steals their time.

"Who are you?" Tam's family asks.

"A friend," Kila responds, as she holds in her crying. *A
love*, she thinks as she tries not to exhale, scared she will
breathe out things instead of air.

And with the chemo comes a world of brown eyes, still
slightly slanted, now with tired wrinkles, small-locked
dreads that fall one at a time to the ground leaving parts of
scalp visible—vulnerable—dimples that never go away—
thank god they never go away— accompanying a smile
that these days leaves for extended periods of time without
notice.

At night, Kila throws up continents. Coming out of her,
they slice her open from the inside out until they are in the
toilet bowl and they become tiny things again. Only totems
of bigger things. She holds on tightly to the sky within her
chest, refusing to let it go.

Kila is scared that if she throws up the stars, she will
lose Tam; she convinces herself it is the only thing that
keeps her tiny big love alive.

One day Tam is coughing up phlegm stuck with tiny
specks of blood on her hospital gown and says to Kila,
"Let us go see the sky."

Kila wants to say, "It is in my chest. I have saved it for
you," but instead she says, "You are not allowed to leave
your room this late at night."

And there is a little twinkle in Tam's eyes but Kila is
not fooled. She knows it is a ball of fire. "Live a little."

When Tam laughs—and Kila will do anything for that

laugh—she says, "If we get caught, they will have more pity on you, so I am going to say I tried to stop you."

Tam says, "You are going to blame the patient. How cruel!"

And they are both holding in their laughs and sneaking through hallways and past nurses falling asleep on desk duty until they are at a balcony on the east wing under the night sky.

"We're not all the way outside." Tam sighs.

"Close enough." Kila wraps her love in her arms and inhales Tam's scent.

Tam touches skin, turns around and lifts fingers to the necklace around Kila's neck. "Tell me again of your grandmother's song?"

As Tam touches the cowrie shell that Kila breathed out when she was five, it glows. Kila does not know if Tam can see it, but the warmth seeps down her neck into her shoulders. "There are so many versions of it."

"We have all the time in the world, baby."

Kila laughs and stops pretending she can hold in her tears. She starts telling the version of the story of the big tribe being protected by a small spirit that lives in the cowrie shell. How the spirit taught the big tribe that time doesn't exist in the conjunction of big and little things.

Tam looks at the stars in the sky. "I think I am going to be a big ball of fire pretending to be a tiny twinkling star."

And Kila thinks *time doesn't exist at the conjunction of big and little things*, so she inhales her tiny big love in and exhales the sky.

Assimilation

Sharang Biswas

Bronze ring of laurels encasing a crimson disk sat on Adam's blazer like a pustule. It celebrated "Extraordinary Sacrifice in Service of Earth-2." Rodrigo had watched the awards ceremony online.

An acid-green bracelet gripped Adam's right wrist, continually transmitting vitals and GPS to Pentagon-2. Looking at it made Rodrigo wince.

While Rodrigo drove, Adam radiated nervous energy. His gaze flicked between the rearview mirror, the dashboard, and the coral sands outside.

The hiss of anxious tension issuing into the car was almost audible.

Fuck it, Rodrigo had to say something. "So...two years on the moon!" he tried. "Could've written, man!"

Adam's eyes darted to him. His tongue flicked, moistening his lips.

There was the dude Rodrigo knew—

"We're permitted little communication," Adam replied. His hands twitched in his lap.

—and there *went* the dude Rodrigo knew. The accent, the inflection, these Rodrigo recognized. But his best friend would never have constructed that sentence. Rodrigo wanted to hit something.

Adam turned away and resumed his jittery examination of the car.

The desert between the airport and New Boston was peppered with rest stops resembling homey log-cabins. Rodrigo hated the ersatz nostalgia.

Silence inflated the car like a balloon, pressing against the two, pushing them apart.

Rodrigo switched on the radio; the song playing nearly made him swerve. Adam had spent the last night before his deployment trying to teach Rodrigo that song. "So we're connected through music, no matter where I am," Adam had said.

Rodrigo switched off the radio.

†

Frank ignored the phone. It was probably for Shalini.

The potatoes weren't right.

Frank had been known for his mashed potatoes back on Old Earth. Golden. Buttery. Melt-in-your-mouth. Dehydrated potato flakes did not achieve the same effect. He fingered his mixing spoon, as though the wood grain held the culinary secrets he needed.

"Adam's coming!!" Aisha's voice shattered the silence like radio static. She sprinted into the kitchen, twirling—her thick plait nearly knocking over the salt—and rushed back out.

Aisha was unique, part of the first generation to be born off-Earth-1. It didn't make raising her any easier.

Frank returned to his mash with vengeance.

When Shalini announced herself with a knock, Frank didn't acknowledge it.

"Rodrigo says they're on their way," Shalini announced.

Frank tasted the potatoes.

"It'll be nice for them to catch up," she continued.

'They used to be inseparable!" The forced cheeriness of her voice did not escape Frank.

He shrugged, adding another tablespoon of TruButter.

"I'm going to tell Aisha," she continued.

Frank put down his spoon.

"Frank, she has a right to know—"

Frank turned to his wife. Her hair was disheveled, he noticed. "She's a child."

"It's the first time she's seeing her brother in two years," Shalini insisted. "And he's not a *criminal* that she needs to be shielded from. He made a sacrifice. He's a *war-hero!* I don't want him to become some sort of...*stranger.*"

Frank turned to the window. Synthetic sunshine bleached away the kitchen's color and emotion.

"He *is* a stranger," Frank said softly. "Why does no one else see that?"

†

Adam's room hadn't changed.

"Familiar?" Rodrigo asked, gesturing around. "Adam's—*your* memories are intact, right?"

His smile slipped at the blank expression Adam gave the wall-mounted guitar.

Adam approached the instrument and fingered the strings. *Plink-Plink-Plink.*

"Assimilation is not perfect," he said, looking up.

Rodrigo wanted to *yank* the guitar out of Adam's hands, wanted to *force* him to play their song. He dumped Adam's bag on the bed. The bedsprings squealed.

Adam's body jerked, as though struck by lightning. His eyes widened. He turned to Rodrigo with a curious expression. "That sound...I remember...bacon and cannabis—"

Shalini's voice from downstairs cut in. "Boys! Dinner!"

Whatever breakthrough Adam had experienced

dissolved. He licked his lips, fidgeted his fingers. His eyes were panicky.

Rodrigo couldn't help it. Despite everything. "Adam! Look at me?"

Adam did.

His eyes were still black, black, *black*. "Caught in my event horizon?" he'd joked that night as Rodrigo had stared into them.

He stared again, this time searching for what lay *behind* those eyes, for the networked bacterial floc that had taken over his best friend's brain, had seized his sentience. That had somehow driven him and a legion of soldiers to a desperate victory at the battle of Zagreus II, that had earned him a fucking *medal* even though—

"Boys!"

Rodrigo coughed. "Look, you'll get through this, okay?"

†

"Potatoes?" Shalini offered.

Frank grunted as Adam accepted a spoonful of greasy starch. Aisha eyed them warily from across the table.

"So have you met any nice girls at Pentagon-2?" Shalini joked. "Must be many smart women up there!"

Adam shot a beseeching look at Rodrigo, who merely squirmed. "We're not allowed," Adam began, "sexual relationships are—"

"Hey!" Frank scowled at Adam and gestured towards his sister. Shalini hastily offered Frank some beans.

Adam looked bewildered.

"Why aren't you eating, Adam?" Aisha chirped.

Shalini gave her a worried look.

"Err…We have to control our lipid intake," Adam ventured. "To regulate neural myelination. It's essential for optimal Assimilation—"

His sister interrupted him. "Is it because of the funny thing in your head?"

Frank stood up in a clatter of cutlery, glaring at Shalini. "I'm going upstairs."

"Frank!" Shalini cried. "You haven't seen your son in two years!"

"That's not my son. Adam was killed by an alien two years ago."

Rodrigo swallowed his potatoes with difficulty.

†

Plink-Plink-Plink

Adam's face scrunched up in concentration.

Rodrigo sat next to him on the bed, hugging his knees. He wanted to grab the guitar, wanted to get it *away* from whoever this was that didn't know how to play it.

Adam stopped strumming. "I did not choose this," he said quietly.

"Huh?"

Adam's eyes were moist. "I did not choose Assimilation."

"How much of Adam is left? How much is the alien?" Rodrigo could feel the hoarseness in his own voice.

Adam bowed his head. "I don't know," he whispered, gripping the neck of the guitar so tightly that his knuckles went white.

Rodrigo uncurled himself. "Hey, man, I'm sorry..." he began but Adam looked up and Rodrigo was caught in the event horizon.

"Rodrigo," Adam intoned, tasting the word in his mouth, feeling the shape his lips made around it: *Rod-REE-go*.

It was the first time Adam had spoken his name since his arrival.

"Rodrigo," Adam repeated, "I remember..."

Something wrung out Rodrigo's stomach, squeezed his windpipe, hammered his heart— because Rodrigo remembered too.

The midnight snack. The joints. How'd he'd got too high to learn the song, how the bedsprings had *squealed*—

"You tasted of bacon and cannabis," Adam said, "and something else I can't describe..."

Rodrigo swallowed.

He looked at the man who had once been his best friend, a man who was now this new creature lost in a world that he was supposed to know but could never really belong to, who was at once intensely familiar and utterly alien.

"Hey." He shuffled over and placed his hands over Adam's fingers. "Want me to teach you how to play that? A friend once told me that music connects us, no matter who we are."

A GIRL PREDICTS
THE FUTURE

RUTH JOFFRE

FOR $1, YOU'LL learn when your mother will next
prepare your favorite dish—in your case, chilaquiles
topped with fried egg and avocado slices, available
either in six weeks and three days or next Saturday
morning, provided that you are patient and ask nicely
after allowing her to sleep until ten a.m. for once in your
life.

For $10, you can ascertain what grade you will receive
on the upcoming history project if you pursue your plan
of compiling an oral history of the migrant farm workers
in your family. As a sign of respect for this choice, I will
tell you for free whether this grade will be impacted by
the teacher's personal beliefs about immigration and the
border wall, beliefs you already find suspect not because
of what Mr. Calvin has said but because of what he has
pointedly avoided saying, all those vast swaths of history
untouched because he did not want to acknowledge U.S.
interference in Latin American politics, for instance, or
the real reason Oklahoma has a panhandle.

For $20, I'll tell you whether you will get the job you
just interviewed for—that interview you told nobody

about, not even your best friend, because you do not
believe in celebrating one's capitulations to capitalism.
You would rather clock in every day after class, wear a
shirt that does not fit, and give nothing of yourself to that
place, not even your name, not even on your nametag,
because no one at that store will be able to pronounce
Xochitl anyway, not unless somebody you know walks
in, which seems unlikely, because your people don't shop
there and your classmates, if they do, will not recognize
you in this context, in what they consider their domain.

For $40, you can preview your first trip overseas, which
will be on vacation, a real vacation in the foothills of
the Andes, where you will breathe the thin, thin air and
amble through cobblestone streets with a cone of helado
de canela, its deep orange color like a papaya's flesh as a
knife slices it down the middle. This, you think, is luxury:
walking beside people who look like you, hearing no
English, allowing the cinnamon sorbet to melt through
your fingers as you pause at a bookstore and browse their
window displays. All those beautiful worlds between
pages. You will never stop daydreaming of places where
you can feel safe.

For $70, I'll tell you a little about the first time you kiss
a girl: what the weather is like on that afternoon, what
shapes the clouds take and what songs the birds sing, and
whether the purple dinosaurs frolicking on her dress are
her own design or a custom commission from a queer
fabric artist she follows on social media, but not what her
name is, not how you meet or when—nothing that could
alter the delicate chemistry of the flirtation as it blossoms
into something more. You will experience this all yourself,
and it will be glorious. Trust me.

For $100, I can allay all your concerns about applying
to college, those nagging questions about whether your
SAT scores are good enough and whether you're reaching
too high or should apply to more safety schools and

whether the fee waivers you requested will be granted,
the toxic messages that if you don't go to college you will
never amount to anything, that this one decision could
mean the difference between meeting that girl and not,
heading to the Andes and not, being happy and not,
to which I will say: none of these things are necessarily
interdependent. Spending $100 here will not kick off a
chain reaction that results in you not being able to afford
to apply to two colleges, which turn out to be the only
ones you would have gotten in to, which thus changes the
course of your entire life. If that were possible, I would
not offer you this information. I can't see what can't come
true, and I'm not in the business of changing the future.

My augury services are all sliding scale, priced not by
the difficulty of the precognition or the seriousness of the
request but by the value of the peace of mind provided
to my customers. In exchange for your $100, you will
receive a window into your future: a perfect moment
of clarity, when all the blocks inside of your brain clear
and you finally allow yourself to believe in a future you
already know is possible. A future you glimpsed in your
dreams but never permitted yourself to embrace, because
you know how this world likes to squash people who look
like you and love like you, you know just how hard it is to
survive (let alone thrive) under such conditions, and you
know, too, that the knowledge of your future happiness is
worth so much more than $100—more than anyone or
anything can ethically charge or afford—but I'm offering
it anyway, because you, Xochitl, deserve some relief.
Enjoy it.

Four Glass Cubes (Item Description)

Bogi Takács

Four glass cubes, with colorful pieces of paper sticking out of them, partially embedded in the material. From the estate of Ms. Eliza Sárásréti.

THE SÁRÁSRÉTI CUBES are some of our most curious acquisitions, created by Ms. Sárásréti, a chartered public accountant employed by local company Silberstein és Tsa., who led a reclusive life, and was during her lifetime not considered an artist of note.

These pieces appear to be cube-shaped blown glass paperweights, of unknown provenance. Pieces of paper cut thin or sometimes torn ostensibly by hand from advertisements and other leaflets have been embedded in the material of each paperweight, in patterns of varying complexity. Some of the cubes resemble hedgehogs, with paper strips and slices haphazardly jutting out of them, while others could be compared to flowers, with the paper elements placed along a logarithmic spiral or some other pattern. The 'hedgehogs' are generally considered earlier work, though the Cubes are difficult to date with precision despite the incorporated print advertisements.

Dozens of them were found in Ms. Sárásréti's home after her passing, mostly in the kitchen and dining area, with some on a living room coffee table. No other exemplars are known.

The mystery of the Cubes lies in their unknown means of production. While embedding paper in transparent epoxy resin is commonly done, embedding paper in glass is not feasible without using custom-made paper, due to the high temperature at which glass melts. None of the necessary apparatus or materials for such were in evidence in Ms. Sárásréti's small townhome, and the paper used was sourced from advertising leaflets. Further, it is unknown whether she constructed the glass paperweights herself or whether she only inserted the strips of paper into premade paperweights.

The currently most accepted theory proposed by Gerard *et al.* states that the Cubes were produced using a psychokinetic process, though there are several facts that seemingly contradict this approach. Ms. Sárásréti was not known to possess any psychokinetic capability— she had been screened twice, at both middle school and high school graduation. No other phenomena of anomalous perturbation were documented to occur in her surroundings. Her townhome was situated in Zone Three, making such highly controlled manifestations unlikely without enormous expenditure of energy. Further, the only available eyewitness testimony (see below) suggests that Ms. Sárásréti made the Cubes herself and by hand, though by an entirely unknown method. Grinfeld *et al.* have noted the similarity of the Cube patterns to some sketches and other marginalia in Ms. Sárásréti's notebooks.

Even though the Cubes are visually striking, to the extent that they have become symbolic of our region, it is unclear if they were produced or intended as art. While some of the artist's watercolor landscapes were shown as part of student group exhibitions at the local arts center, she never made the Cubes available for public display or sale.

Ms. Sárásréti lived alone and never married; according to her social media profiles, she described herself as an asexual lesbian. She occasionally dated, but never invited her dates to her home. The only person who witnessed the Cubes during Ms. Sárásréti's lifetime was her neighbor and friend Ms. Renáta Berger-Udvardy. According to Ms. Berger-Udvardy, the Cubes were "just haphazardly lying around in her kitchen, I always assumed they were part of an unfinished crafts project of some sort, or maybe Christmas ornaments." (The Christmas ornament theory can be safely rejected based on the available evidence that Ms. Sárásréti belonged to a small, close-knit Traditional Egalitarian Jewish congregation, and was not known to observe Christmas.) Ms. Berger-Udvardy also claimed to have witnessed Ms. Sárásréti "poking little rolled-up pieces of paper into the cubes, just by hand." No accompanying visual or auditory phenomena, or unexpected temperature changes, were observed. Both the cubes and the pieces of paper appeared to remain solid throughout the construction process, though Ms. Berger-Udvardy admitted "not paying especially close attention."

Kovács and Mihajlovics proposed that the Cubes might have been produced as part of so-called "stimming" behaviors often demonstrated by persons on the autism spectrum, not as art for display; underscored by the fact that Ms. Berger-Udvardy observed Ms. Sárásréti work on the Cubes while carrying on a conversation, an activity with social components that could presumably be stressful. However, Kanalas *et al.* noted that nothing precluded autistic artists from enjoying their work the same as neurotypical artists would. Nyáray *et al.* reviewed available evidence for Ms. Sárásréti's neuroatypicality and noted it to be scant; they also offered an alternate interpretation in favor of attention deficit disorder. We note that some replicas offer removable and reattachable slice segments, and these have seen an enthusiastic uptake as stim toys, despite some of their characteristics making this activity somewhat hazardous (see later).

Jameson and Roberts offered a popular interpretation that the Cubes were intended as an ironic, deconstructive take on Rubik's Cubes, but Kanalas *et al.* rejected this interpretation as one based on American stereotypes about Hungary. Further argument against this theory is that two tetrahedral paperweights were also found, of the 'hedgehog' type, in the Sárásréti estate; making "Cubes" as a term itself somewhat of a misnomer. Another theory expressed by Gregg *et al.* considers them a similar deconstruction of "rainbow capitalism"—here, a speculative parallel can be drawn with the fact that plastic replicas of the Cubes have proliferated widely in recent years, in part due to them being read as a symbol of homegrown queer resistance. (The intra-community controversy over whether Ms. Sárásréti could be called a "patron saint" is discussed at length by Székely and Salamon.) The overt queerness of Cubes has been contested, e.g., see in Istvánhegyessy *et al.*, mostly in relation to appeals to traditionalism. A widely reported court case determined the Cubes did not fall under the remit of laws restricting homosexual propaganda.

One must note that the edges and corners of Cubes are unusually sharp; this characteristic tends to be maintained across replicas.

Together

Iori Kusano

THE LOVE SHINO always wanted would have been warm and soft, melting spun-sugar sweet on the tongue.

What she's got is this clawing thing, jagged with broken-mirror edges, and she's going to hold it close all the way down.

It's going to break her open, spill her out like a jar of preserves smashed on the counter.

She doesn't much mind, anymore.

†

IF SHINO REACHES back like she's trying to scratch an itch, she can just touch the port between her shoulder blades. It does itch, sometimes. She can't sleep nude anymore, either; she's got to wear a t-shirt or else her long hair makes the skin around it tickle.

She could cut her hair, but it's one of the things she likes about this body, her third in the last five years. Nao picked it out for her after the last one got ruined.

What was that like, anyway? Flipping through the vessel files in the director's office together, her datachip on a lanyard around Nao's neck, skin-warmed. She would have walked down to the lab, nodding, pointing, *that one.*

Shino knows what it's like. She did it too for Nao, once. She's just making conversation.

†

YOU'RE NOT BIG enough for both of us.

It's her thought and Nao's at the same time now—all boundaries between them eroded. They're blended together like a sick sweet smoothie, have been from the moment Shino decided she wouldn't wait any longer for Nao's next body. Choosing was the easy part; the nightmare of procedure, of paperwork, of payouts and checkups and *sign here please* before she was allowed to restore from backup had been the loneliest year of her life. She couldn't face it twice.

Now they'll reload together, every time.

I never asked you for this, I never wanted this, I never, I never—

Yeah, but Nao? No matter what happens now, I'll never have to live a single day without you.

She wraps her arms around herself, nails digging into her biceps, and she doesn't know if she's trying to rip herself open or stroke herself calm.

CUBICLE REFUGIA

JACKSON JESSE NASH

ITCHING BIOLOGY, MY favorite class, to take a call at 9 a.m. American time, 2 p.m. my time. The boy's toilets in the sixth form block at school, and not a soul there but me and the spiders. The crack in the stall barrier between this cubicle and the next had long ago become a fault line threatening to reveal too much, whichever side you sat on. The small slit of a high window let a brief, blinding slice of sunlight cut across me, dissecting me in UV, before blinking out behind a cloud. The real ditchers were out smoking weed behind the hill, or sniffing poppers, drinking vodka. Maybe filling balloons with nitrous oxide. It was worth ditching to take a phone call from Hank McCaw. I'd rather that be my reason than just plain old getting fucked up.

This time last week in biology we'd learned about cryptic refugia—areas of warmth surrounded by ice sheets in the Last Glacial Maximum that miraculously allowed some species to survive. There was nothing cryptic about the graffiti in here. Cocks, tits, diagrams with arrows pointing to *clit*. Insults like *sea punks suck*. Above a phone number, the word *Shag*. A million standard *<insert name>* woz *'ere* tags, like this was just some innocent and out-of-touch kid's comic from the 1950s. I hoped the bullies with sling shots and rockabilly quiffs weren't about to burst into my cubicle refugia, bringing the chill of the past and present into this warm pocket of time.

The phone vibrated in my hand.

"Hi, is this ██████?"

Like any good UFO story I've redacted my name from this document, my girl name. ██████ *woz 'ere.* A sudden thudding in the corridor and past the loo entrance made me hold my breath for an instant before I could answer, but whoever it was hurried on late to class.

"This is Hank McCaw." As though I wouldn't recognize that husky voice from the Appalachian mountains. I listened to *The McCaw Report* every week like my life depended on it. Sacred geometry, unidentified aerial phenomenon, crop circles and golden ratios. The kind of guest speakers known as cereologists, ufologists, others who believed that the government, no, *all* governments, were hiding the real extent of human encounters with extraterrestrial life. I never expected him to email me back, let alone call me, but there he was, Hank McCaw, connected to my phone. I shifted on the lid of the loo, my arse sliding on the cool, smooth surface.

Hank's deep voice, a raspy edge like the beginning of a tiny fracture in an iceberg, explained the recording process. I made affirmative noises, not really taking it in, feeling my heart thump just to be on the phone with him.

I began rambling, nervously at first, about how the lights weren't orbs the way you always hear people describe, how they were longer, more like cylinders.

"Start with how you got there," he said. I had been out there in the field at 1 a.m. It felt good to sneak out and have time alone on the dark roads of the village while my family slept, to become a nameless entity darting behind an allotment, through holes in fences in the cold of the night. Overgrown bushes scratched at my skin, causing

hot lines to rise up, pinpricking blood. The aerial photo
had been all over the local news just that afternoon—two
large circles joined by three parallel lines. Smaller circles
and wavy lines formed an intricate border of swirling
constellations. When I found the right field, the sky
above it seemed to be as much cable as it was sky, pylons
stretching forever across the countryside. My spiky hair
mimicked aerials that tried to reach out to those cables, to
connect me to searing wires and thick metal.

The rhythmic crackle of the wheat bled sound from
my soles into the farmland. My chest tightened when
I reached the largest circle, my breathing reduced to
a shallow whisper. Those night-damp stalks had given
under the pressure of whatever—whoever—made the
circles. They'd been tested almost to breaking point,
roots desperately holding on to the Earth. I wondered if
they would be forced to measure out the rest of their lives
horizontally. Grass-dwelling creatures of unknown taxa
scurried far away amidst the occasional eerie snippets of
birdsong. A booming thud shook the ground and my body
vibrated. A *ksssht* like paper tearing as the wheat parted
somewhere nearby—

—Above me in the loo, the spiders spun their own
patterns, too many to count. Fat drops of water hung from
the moldy pipes, never quite managing to fall.

"It got freezing then, really cold." Hank made a sound,
as if this was exactly what he expected me to say. "I was in
the center of the largest circle after moving through some
of its constellations. I felt this pressure, like I might be
flattened as low as the crops. And that was when I saw the
lights above me. White and red, the cylinders."

I told him how they seemed to dart too fast in insectoid
spurts, then halt dramatically. How they seemed to be
miles above me and then in seconds as low as the pylons
and power lines as though they might rain down on me,
shower me in light.

"Then I heard the wheat parting again, and this thudding like the footsteps of some huge animal." I told him about the glimpse of the figure in the rustling stalks, how it looked too small to make so much noise. The featureless face. The shape almost exactly my own, only stretched out with spikes that grew up and up, fading into the night.

"Now, ███████, you know that on this show we like to look at things from all angles, particularly the skeptical. Our listeners might be thinking the lights were just a plane, or maybe…" and he went on with explanations of why what I was saying might be a mistake, an untruth.

He asked me what I'd say to the skeptics. A shadow darted across the window slit, and the briefest flash of red then white flickered through the cracked stall. The skeptical would explain that away as a bird, a trick of the light. I took a marker out of my bag and began writing on the wall by the fault line. *Ben woz 'ere. Stephen woz 'ere. Clive, Michael, phoenix, Jeff.* I tried out the names one by one to see if any of them were mine.

"███████? Are you still there?" I let the silence hang a little longer.

"No," I said, gently pressing the *end call* symbol.

I drew a circle round the name I liked best, connecting it with three parallel lines to the break in the wall. The shadow crept under the door, spikes slowly lengthening to meet me.

OCEAN CHRISTENING

KARYN DE FREITAS

*A*NANSI HAD CHOSEN a sheltered inlet on the east coast for the ritual. The inlet gave access to the cold Atlantic while offering privacy and protection from the worst of the night surf. Anansi had been here during the day. They knew all about the flags, flapping from bamboo poles, the piles of flowers. The inlet was a place of spiritual importance for various religious groups, particularly popular among the Shouter Baptists and the Hindus. Local myth claimed that the cave at the Northern end of the inlet was home to a mermaid, and that if you brought a special enough offering, the mermaid might grant a wish. Not many ventured inside, and those who did refused to speak of what they saw. Anansi wasn't sure what they believed, but they figured that if there was a chance of the mermaid being real, they might as well be respectful.

Anansi loved stories. Growing up, their father would tell them stories before bed. Stories about Papa Bois or folktales, such as the one that explained why the turtle had a cracked shell. They always found themselves drawn to the tricksters. Loki, with his genderfluidity, was particularly special to Anansi, but they were not of that culture.

It was a gamble to show up without material goods, but Anansi hoped to offer something else. Their sister was napping in their car, just a short walk away from the beach. They hoped that if something went wrong, she would hear and be able to help. As much as Anansi knew that this moment was a personal one, that their sister agreed to accompany them in the dead of night to perform the ritual meant more than they could ever fully express. After taking a moment to breathe in deeply and center themself, Anansi was ready to begin.

The moon hung low in the sky, looming large overhead and illuminating the strip of beach where Anansi stood. A Pierrot Grenade costume lay discarded on the damp sand, its many strips of coloured cloth fluttering in the sea breeze. In the pale light, the inlet's rocks seemed sharper and more jagged, while lighter colours, such as the foaming waves, glowed ethereally. Anansi turned towards the candles they had stuck to. For this ritual, Anansi had placed a black candle, a blue candle, and a white candle on the rocks, near to where the waves were breaking. The colours just seemed right for what they were about to do, though in the moonlight, the darker candles looked black while the white candle glowed.

Focusing on the calm rhythm to the ebb and flow of the water, Anansi could feel the song within them swell to a new urgency. They lit the three candles.

The song changed within them once again; it was time. They took a deep breath before wading into the breaking waves. They paid attention to the pull of the water, mindful of the possibility of seaward currents, even in this sheltered area. As they bobbed in the water, the ground not too far below their feet, Anansi closed their eyes and focused on the song. It had no words, and was sometimes a hum, sometimes a cacophony of sound, always strongest near the sea. The song filled Anansi's with this invisible symphony and the more they focused, something within them expanded.

A conch shell sounded. All was still, as if nature itself held its breath after that sound. The deep bellow startled Anansi's eyes open. They were no longer alone. A feminine figure with long locs floated less than a foot away, her dark skin taking on a bluish hue in the moonlight. Anansi swiped their hand across their face to make sure they weren't seeing things. The mermaid's eyes seemed bottomless in the ghostly light. Her lips stretched into a smile, revealing row upon row of pointy teeth. Anansi instantly thought of sharks. It took all of their effort to maintain their composure.

The mermaid spoke without changing her toothy grin, directly into Anansi's mind. *Yuh different. What yuh want?* Images of gold or filled fishing nets flashed in Anansi's mind, offers of what the mermaid could give.

Anansi shook their head. "I want you to witness something." They were painfully aware of the effort it took to remain afloat as they watched the mermaid's stillness. The mermaid's expression remained inscrutable, but she hadn't tried to drown Anansi yet, so they pressed their point. They tried to share a series of memories—stories—with the mermaid, unsure of exactly how to express their thoughts. There was a flutter of excitement from the mermaid as she observed what Anansi shared with them.

I witness your testimony. Wait here, they commanded, before disappearing beneath the surface of the water.

Anansi complied but couldn't shake the feeling that they were at the mercy of the mermaid. The thought of being dragged beneath the water did not leave their mind.

After several minutes, however, the mermaid returned. *This is for you.* The mermaid approached Anansi with a small shell.

Anansi accepted it graciously, tucking it into their binder, where it wouldn't get lost. "Thank you."

Go forth Anansi, child of the sea.

The mermaid's head sank slowly into the water until she was no longer visible, not even a ripple to tell of her recent presence. Anansi could no longer sense another consciousness at the periphery of their own. They were alone with the stars again.

Stories were already churning in Anansi's mind as they swam back to shore. They stood dripping on the sand and looked up at the stars. They'd been prepared for only those glowing points of light to witness them. They felt for the shell tucked into their binder. The sea's blackness was as opaque as it had always been, but Anansi could feel the mermaid's song, the enduring song, and their heart felt full knowing that their renaming had been witnessed. This experience would also become a song or a poem. They left their costume and the still-burning candles, climbing up the incline to their sister and the car they both shared. Anansi smiled as they watched her for a moment, then knocked on the car window.

Their sister jolted awake and unlocked the doors. "How was it?" she asked, yawning widely.

"Good."

"What should I call you now?"

"Anansi?"

"Alright Anansi, lewe go home."

ʃAKEBOYS

Sean Chua

1.

I tell him he's too good to hold down; he spreads so much, extends himself too far for the taking. The boy sighs and lays his head on my lap, black tresses forming pools across my thighs. It's the last day of the last break we'll ever get before graduation, before life as we know it will evaporate into so many applications and deadlines— but for now the afternoons are hot and sweet, and the grass smells of sweat before it rains, and all the land is held in suspension between our skins. My gaze resting on his forehead, forever.

2.

Difficult to keep things still in this moving country— he's changed his number twice, his address three times— but I find him in the woods, spread between the leaves, threading the morning light in between his teeth. He's right to keep his distance, but we're far enough from town for it to not matter. When the wind rises it'll take us and half the damn forest with it anyway. When I step into the clearing he leaps and lets me catch him on my tongue. Given the distance it's a wonder he lets me at all.

3.

HE'S BIG ENOUGH to fill a city—doesn't give a name, but I well believe he could. Off the coast we pick pretty rocks out of flotsam and match them with each other. The storm's a few days out but I'm betting we'll survive. We link arms on the jetty, dancing over each other's shadows, and when I stumble over the planks he laughs. He offers me a stick in apology. I think of how easily he could crush me. When I press my head to his chest I hear a subterranean roar.

4.

DAYS SPENT POUNDING nails to windowsills. Nights spent huddling in the basement. It's only his father's wrath, what are you gonna do about it, I joke, and we just need to tide ourselves through this one terrifying week. This boy's all wind and hot air, doesn't have much of a frame to him, he's calm on the surface but I can hear his breathing through his neck. We hold each other tightly when the wind shrieks his name. When it passes, we emerge from the hatch and his clouds light up seven colours all the way from here to the corner store.

5.

I'LL ONLY KNOW this when I'm older—the water has always been here and it will always find a place to settle down. Different shapes and colours and depths but the going stays the same. Tonight I dissolve into another pair of open arms.

FREQUENTLY ASKED QUESTIONS ABOUT THE DEAD WOMAN BENEATH SANG-D'HELOISE SUBWAY STATION

Ann LeBlanc

1) How do I find her?

DESCEND THE STAIRS to the northbound platform. Trail your finger across the cracked mosaic wall, lingering on the faded jellyfish for good luck. At the far end of the platform, the orange barrier reads *Danger: Electrified Tracks*. Pretend you are there to catch a train. Wait.

When the last car of the train leaves the platform, slip under the barrier, down the service ladder, and into the tunnel. You have five minutes—if you're lucky, if it's not rush-hour—before the next train comes. Hurry.

Walk along the tracks, keeping your right hand against the grease-grime tunnel wall, avoiding the third rail to your left. Bring no light with you; ensure you are not followed. We cannot afford to move her again.

Keep going. It's farther than you think, harder to reckon distance down in the hot dark wetness as adrenaline pounds the locked door of your heart. Walk until you reach the rust-iron door tagged with the face of the nameless martyr. Knock five times.

Wait in the dark until your soul screams you cannot wait any longer. The door will open with a blast of air, dry and cool. Enter quickly; lock the door behind you.

Let your eyes adjust. Do not flinch when you see the
corpse sprawled out on a stained and tattered recliner.
Call her by her name: Aya.

2) Does she take insurance? Do I need payment?

NO. BRING NOTHING but your hopes, your questions, the
desperate yearning needs you dress yourself up in late at
night when no-one is there to react in horror to the parts
of you they call a monster (the corpse will tell you the
truth: you are not a monster).

3) Where did she come from?

THIS IS THE story the corpse will tell you:

Aya was born atop a craggy pine-covered mountain that
rose out of the desert plain like a tumor. When she died,
they laid her body in a crypt carved into the mountain so
the thin dry air would preserve her.

When she was newly dead, the living would come on
her birthday, sweep away the dust, and string her crypt
with flowers. They would eat and drink, sing and laugh,
and ask for her advice.

Most precious of these petitioners were those who—like
she had done herself—transitioned from one role, one
body to another. The words back then were different, but
today we call us trans, nonbinary, queer.

She cared for them, her people within the people. She
led them down the path she had already walked, gifting
them the words and names they needed, the knowledge of
herbs and unguents and knife-cuts to make their bodies
cleave to their souls.

Centuries passed, the rains moved, the people changed
and forgot. Aya thought that she might perform her
service forever—death being constant, unchanging—but
the world changed around her until one day there was
nothing outside her crypt but sand and ruin. She slept.

When she awoke, two eons later, her body was pinned

to the wall like a lepidopterist's butterfly. Small children
and harried mothers gazed at her from the other side of
the glass. She might have been content to remain there in
the natural history museum except for two things.

First, the curators had affixed a label to her: *Male preserved
copse, sessile, late thistle era.* An impossible insult. Second, as
the visitors watched her, she watched them. She recognized
us, hiding within oversized hoodies, looking downward,
avoiding the gazes of others that told us our bodies didn't
fit.

She was needed, and so when the guests departed and
the guards dozed, she crashed through the glass and strode
out to wander the dark and noisome places of the city. The
curators called it an inexplicable theft. They hunt her still.

4) Is that true?

DOES IT MATTER? The stories the powerful tell about us
are more real to them than the truths we speak with our
bodies. Tell your own story; never dull the keen edge of it
for their sake.

5) What services does she provide?

IF YOU ARE reading this—perhaps on a creased pamphlet
gifted to you by someone who has already walked the
path you so desperately want to follow, or perhaps on a
dim computer screen, tilted away so no-one will see—then
surely you already have some hint of what you seek?

Perhaps you are new to the path, or perhaps you were
under the care of a doctor when the new laws passed.
Aya—and her priests—will provide everything the
doctors and therapists and surgeons provided, but not like
they did. She is one of us and knows us and loves us like
they never did.

6) What should I wear?

WRAP YOURSELF IN whatever clothes will safeguard your

heart. Aya is two eons old and has no understanding of the messages encoded in cloth and fit. She cares more about your words and your will than wool and linen.

7) Will she accept me? Am I trans/nonbinary enough?

YES.

8) How can I help?

DONATIONS ARE ALWAYS appreciated. In particular, we need:

- Dehumidifiers, the better to keep Aya preserved.
- Medical supplies (alcohol wipes, syringes, gauze, etc).
- Medicine (vials of estradiol valerate, testosterone undecanoate, spironolactone, etc)
- Priests. Fill out the contact form and our volunteer coordinator will be in touch.

But what Aya needs most of all is a world where you and her do not have to hide, where she could offer you help in the light of day (perhaps in the botanical garden where the wind-weaving pines of her homeland grow).

So call your alderman, demand they repeal the laws that seek to cut us neatly out of the fabric of society. Sing proudly upon the marble steps of the assembly house; storm their offices; slice yourself upon their paper-strewn desks so they might see the blood their bloodless laws will shed.

Make them understand that we exist, we have always existed, and will not vanish silently because they desire their profit to remain peaceful. We intend to thrive, and if the dead themselves rise up to aid us, and the future holds the promise of our descendants' transition, then how can they hope to prevail against us? We are building our salvation down in the dark beneath the roar of the subways.

We hope you will join us.

Three true Auguries and a Lie

Lauren Bajek

F AR FAR ABOVE, celestial sharks wheeled imperceptibly slowly; schools of comet-bright fish scudded across the night. The Royal Augur adjusted her telescope and bent to inspect the flank of a silvertip shark, which arced across the northwest quadrant of the sky.

"A pattern of scarring and scrapes, consistent with coordinated attack," she said. "You walk a minefield. Quarter twist, with underside of jaw and topside of tail both visible: there is great danger in misjudging who your enemies are."

The King stood with her head tipped back, dark curls foaming down across her shoulders and back, the crimson robes of office falling languorously from her shoulders. She had been born under the shadow of the silvertip shark; at twenty-three, she was new-crowned and in the midst of her first Patron Return.

"That sounds about right," she said. Her voice was low and smooth. "And that's a shyshark and a frilled shark on its tail. Who's born under those shadows, again?"

It was a long list. The Augur wrote their names down, and handed them to the King, who tossed it onto the

Augur's overflowing desk. "Let's go to bed."

Several hours later, the Augur awoke and disentangled herself from the King's long, sweaty limbs. She could never sleep well with the smell of sex on her. She washed her hands and brushed her teeth, then padded back to the telescope.

There, barely visible above the southern horizon, she found it: the great shadow of a whale, on its centuries-long journey back into influence.

Quietly, in her throat, the Augur sang the whalesong her grandmother had taught her. A mournful hopeful almost-tune.

A prayer.

As they always did, the whales counseled patience.

The Augur spun the telescope toward a meaningless part of the sky and returned to bed.

†

ON HER THIRTY-FIRST birthday, the King came for her first augury since ceremonially departing the Augur's bed. ("I have to think of marriage, and heirs; I can't be distracted"—but the Augur knew about Lady Aegrit. And didn't care.)

"The mountain-people are causing trouble again," the King said. "What fate is coming in on the sky-tide?"

"King, they still follow the whale-ways, and orcas have been sighted in the sky. To them, it means…change. Disruption, for good or for bad."

The King waved her hand. "Yes, yes. But do they plan something silly like revolution? It would be a shame to have to stage another genocide."

The Augur hid her shaking hands in the pockets of her apron. She thought of her grandmother, with her strong, twisted knuckles, who had taught her the whalesongs. Her mountain-born cousins, who could jump up the side of a cliff as nimbly as goats, and always teased her for her city manners and sharkly ways. The baby, who she hadn't gotten a chance to meet yet.

"There will be no violence, my King. It's just one sighting, and unconfirmed—anyway, no whale-worshipper would follow an orca into battle. They're not real whales—just dolphins who have gotten wise enough to be dangerous."

The King sighed in relief and clapped the Augur on the shoulder. (Their first physical contact for almost a year. Her smell—)

"Fuck, but I'm glad I can trust you, my little translator. Alright, I'll offer them a political marriage. My sister Ren, maybe. She's not doing me much good moping around the palace. We'll make a big fuss about it. And I'll ready the guns just in case. Now—come here, darling, a kiss for my birthday."

After, the Augur touched her trembling mouth and said, "Would you like to know what a whale-worshipper would see in the sky for you? A little trivia for your birthday."

"Tell me."

"They would tell you that you will have the moon."

That cocky smile flashed across the King's face. "Prosperity and righteous might? I'll take that."

†

At thirty-three, the King asked for advice on her marriage. "My sister's gone and converted to whale-worship, stupid girl. Stupid me, for expecting better of her. Anyway, I've got to produce more babies than she can possibly assassinate. What does the sky say?"

This is the moment, the Augur thought. The current turns here. She sang a little prayer in her throat.

The sky was full of sharks; there were many suitors for a King who was young, beautiful, and famously voracious in bed, even if she ruled over difficult times.

"Do you know you hum when you're thinking?"

The Augur jerked up. "What?"

The King was stroking her own collarbones; flirting. "You always have. It's cute."

No time for that. The Augur returned to the sky. There—a bramble shark with pitted skin across its belly, and crossed behind it, a sleek, fat shape, barely visible in the deepness of the sky. The Augur racked her brain. Who had been born under the bramble shark's fleeting shadow? Ah yes.

"Lord Graecl. The Royal Perfumer's son."

The King wrinkled her brow. "Really? He's unappealing, unconnected, and barely even—"

The Augur cut her off with a raised hand. (Borderline treasonous, but she had to take advantage of the King's brief uncertainty.) "Look. Do you see how the body of the bramble shark arcs in parallel with the body of your divine Patron as it leaves our sphere of the sky? He is aligned with your interests, but secondary to you; he will never outshine you or even try. And he stands in double trine with four other sharks: though apparently insignificant, he is the key to greater power. He will give you the future you hunger for."

The hungry King wavered, set her chin, nodded. "I'll say I'm honoring our tradespeople. And at least I'll smell nice."

You always smell nice, the Augur thought. But the King was gone.

†

AGAINST THE WISHES of her surgeon, with the blood of her hysterectomy still not dry on the mop-rags, the King called the Augur to her side. "What happened?" she croaked. "You hand-picked Graecl for me, but he was carrying the disease that did—this. He mutilated me. And now my sister and her husband will put a line of dirty whale-lovers on the throne."

The Augur said nothing. She hated blood, the smell of it, the way it worked into everything, horrible red-brown grit. She'd been so careful that there would be no blood. (She'd been naive. There's always blood.)

She hummed in her throat, but the whalesong didn't soothe her.

Well, she'd made herself the other kind of whale, hadn't she? The liar. The black-and-white trickster. The killer.

Where would she go, now that her task was done? Not home; no whale would welcome an orca in.

The King gripped her arm with a feverish strength. "Are you listening? I was supposed to have the moon! Instead I get my guts carved out, my kingdom fucked to pieces by my idiot sister, my legacy amputated and left to rot on the surgery floor?"

"Do you know what whale-worshippers say about the moon?" the Augur asked. She felt as cold and remote as the ever-swimming stars.

The King spat on the gory floor. "Of course I don't."

"We say it is the orca's devouring mouth."

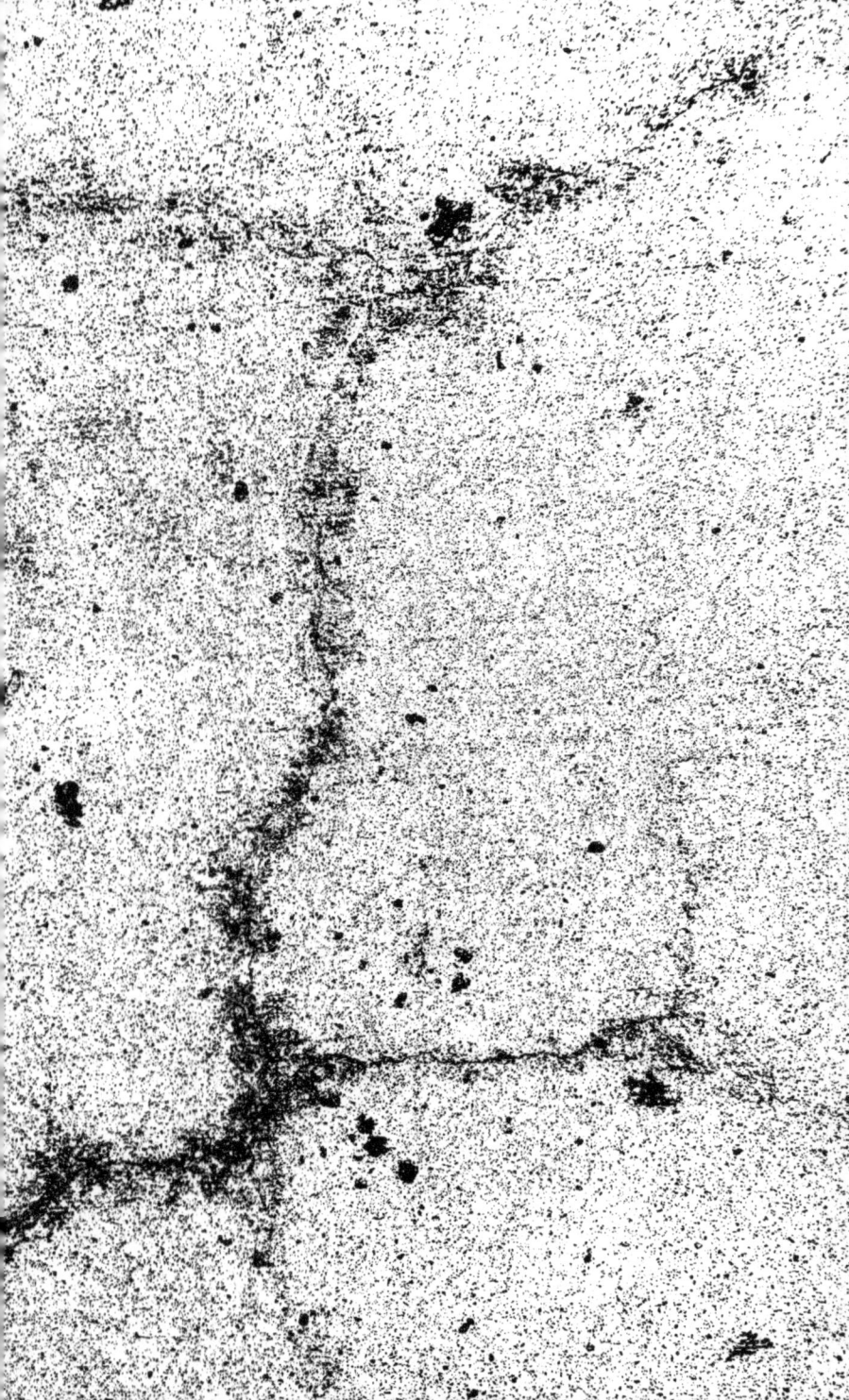

THE SERPENT CROUCHES IN THE HEART OF THE UNRAVELLING

FRUZSINA PITTNER

T HE SERPENT CURLS around the engine core when you enter.

That's not how it starts—you remember, as much as memory can be reliable so close to the heart of the unravelling, the moment linear time and Newtonian physics go tits up for good: Deck 3, Hydroponics, 78% spatial-temporal degradation. Security officer Tahl looking directly at the tree-shaped thing despite your repeated warnings and his skin spiralling off like a peeled tangerine, a body suspended mid-air in zero gravity with its fleshy parts blooming from its spinal column. A delicate structure. Strange. Beautiful, in a way.

You told him.

You *told* him.

"They never listen," you say, and the detailed hallucination of Helen clutching the handhold beside you nods solemnly in understanding.

The fabric of space-time doesn't quite recover after that.

The Serpent is a young, hungry thing. You pull yourself down the elevator shaft toward the belly of the liveship *Fortunate Orbit* when it happens—it takes a beat, a sideways lurch, a *wrongness*. A fissure. The Serpent hums its song, and lights fracture around the periphery of your vision into a technicolour hum. Time turns upside down with a sickening crunch. You swallow around the inside of your body, and *then*—

[you're wiping the remains of officer Tahl off your jumpsuit, you're yelling at Manager Juno, you're shutting your locker for the last time before your reassignment, you're kissing Helen goodbye the morning after and she smiles into it, her nose against your nose a soft pressure, months ago, now, an age,]

Stop it, you think. Your mouth doesn't move. Witchcraft is less about what you say, anyway, and when you relocate your body enough to finally see, you find yourself hovering in front of the hatch to the engine chamber, space-grade metal burst open like overripe fruit. Ribboning wires and titanium alloy curl around you as you pass through.

The Serpent watches.

The Serpent waits.

The Serpent curls around the engine core when you *traverse*, its fat, many-toothed body nothing like any snake you've ever seen, and you're grateful for an absent second that officer Tahl finished dying hours ago: his death would have been worse if he was here and looking at the thing itself instead of *around* it. Unspeakably so.

[He should have listened,] the Serpent offers.

"They never do," you say. Your nose is bleeding again. "Have you been returned before, or am I going to have to go over the specifics?"

[That's very sweet,] the Serpent says with a perversion of fondness that crawls into you like your body is a nest, a shelter.

You brace yourself. Your scanning spell begins emitting a high-pitched shrieking noise. *Spatial degradation 93%,* it says, as the Serpent *opens*—an eye or a thousand, a black-hole gut, a mouth—and all the bones in your body are unmade.

Time lurches again. You're sitting

*[on your mother's balcony, watching the crowd underneath you
ripple and churn like an ocean. on Sister Ludovika's sofa before she
grins toothlessly and sends you into your first unravelling. in the café
by the window overlooking the desert as the proximity notification
from the dating app goes off and you look up to see—]*

Helen. Helen. Helen. Helen in the café. Helen in your
kitchen. Helen in your bed. Helen a month ago, hand
clenched around her duffel's fraying strap.

Her face in your memory is vivid, even greyish and tired
in the half-light ten minutes before the artificial sunrise of
Habitat 7. "Just some space, Fee, for a little while," she says,
mouth curling into a final sort of frown.

Another eye, open.

"You do know you're cursed, right?" you ask—a
sickening turn of memory, a coolness as the Serpent sorts
through time in the fleshy bits of your mind—and you're
back in your apartment with the woman you picked up
online blinking up at you, shirt half-unbuttoned and hair
spilling onto your pillow. You need to do laundry. You
need to get the Serpent to stop *picking memories* for you.

"I'm sorry?" Helen asks, and the curse is a dark,
pulsing, oil spill-shimmer inside her ribcage.

You break it. You always do.

You need to stop thinking about—

[Ah,] says the Serpent, *[how shocking.]*

You splinter back into reality with a wet inhale. The
Fortunate Orbit pulls itself around you in pieces.

[You've always had a weakness for the messy, sad ones,] the
Serpent adds, contemplative. Its form shifts in nauseating
heaves as mass and matter rearrange themselves in front
of you until it takes the shape of—the *wrong* shape, dark
skin and dark eyes and braids and hands but all messed
up, a mockery of a woman that lives in the corners of your
body. Used to. It makes you—something, it turns you *into*
something, the image.

[Can you be a little angrier? It's almost enough, now...]

And you feel it pull you. *Spatial degradation,* says a spell half-disintegrated, but the number is blurry. Unimportant.

"Nah," you say. It's a good enough approximation even if your mouth and your teeth and your vocal cords are occupying different corners of the room as the Serpent pulses and seethes, its body—her body—stretching to end you. Unbirth you.

"This is going to hurt," you add, then allow yourself to lose all remaining form as you cast.

Witchcraft is a matter of depth, not complexity. What is it you need? A piece of string. A tub of bones. A pair of pliers. Everything else is a thought-game.

The spiralling explosion of the Serpent's rage is like nails on a chalkboard: horrid, unavoidable, satisfying. It kicks you in the frontal lobe one last time before you shove its remaining bits through an opening you make in the unravelling. Its face, made wrong, smiles at you with an upside-down mouth and Helen's accusing eyes, warm, terrible.

[I'll be seeing you, bone-eater,] it says, soft like a caress, the last twinge of a persistent headache beneath your skull. *[I hope she never calls you. I hope—]*

You plaster a curse onto the eight-fingered hand that holds onto your form still until it sizzles, spasms, and lets go.

"Okay," you say, then lick your thumb and fuse the opening between space and unspace shut.

†

SHE'S WALKING AWAY from your apartment door when you stumble into the building. You're sweating in the humid, pulsing heat that sits on the rings of Habitat 7.

Spinning up the unravelling took forever. You're desperate for dinner and a nap. You're desperate for a *shower,* truly, but Helen is *here*—here in this mildew-choked house, your house, dipped in shadow enough that her expression is blurred, incomprehensible.

The image of a creature stuffing itself into her memory-shell sits in your mouth, still undigested.

"Hey." Helen says. She shuffles her feet. "I was just passing by, and I thought——"

And that——isn't that just *it?* Helen, thinking. Too much, not enough, about the wrong kinds of things, all the time.

Helen. Here. Again.

"I have noodles," you say, and lift the takeout bag.

You wonder if she'll notice that you still buy her favourite order without thinking, every time.

A GIRL LESS ORDINARY

E.C. BARRETT

WHEN JULIET PEELS off her skin at night, leaving it crumpled beside the bed, I beg her to teach me how. She says she's trying. Then she pads across the mattress on suddenly luminous hands and knees and slides her long square fingers down my thighs. When she slips them inside me, I forget what I was asking.

If I push it, she'll get bored and leave me. And then I'll never know what I'm worth.

†

THE FIRST TIME Juliet unskinned, strips of gossamer peeling away, we danced until last call and she told me she loved me as I fumbled with my keys in the door.

I wrapped her discarded skin in the tablecloth and hid it as she slept, even though she asked me to throw it out. I couldn't stand the thought of it rotting in a pile of soiled diapers, broken dishes and maggot-filled meat.

The maggots would love her skin. I couldn't take it.

Underneath her skin with its deep brown freckles, she
is the subterranean cavern looking into the penguin tank
at the zoo: shimmery, mottled, furtive. I want to dip my
fingers into the murky darkness beneath her skin and lick
my hands clean until I've taken in enough of her that I too
am a marvel, a girl less ordinary.

†

ON SHEDDING NIGHTS, I wait until Juliet's asleep and creep
around the foot of the bed to scoop up her skin and carry it
to the kitchenette. I fill our biggest Pyrex bowl with warm
water and let the skin float on top. I light candles, swirl the
skin with my finger so the flame reflects off the peaks and
valleys of the slowly spinning folds, an opalescent galaxy.

A few drops of oil in the water, bergamot and vetiver,
transport me, and I am her devotee performing a ritual of
preservation.

Juliet's skin has amazing wicking properties, hangs
dry in seconds. I fold it, smoothing it as I go so it won't
wrinkle, and wrap it in one of my shirts, because paper
seems too vulgar. I tuck it away in a box beside the others.
I'm up to ten.

I tried pulling one on, thinking maybe that would teach
me how, but my toes busted through and the whole thing
turned to dust.

†

I ASKED HER once if she'd taken off her skin in front of
anyone else. She pouted red-stained lips at me, pulled
my shirt over my head and wrapped it around my wrists,
kissing my neck into gooseflesh.

It was a stupid question, and even though I know it
shouldn't matter, the unspoken answer makes me feel even
less special.

†

It's selfish, her not teaching me. She'd rather keep me a
disciple, bent-kneed and worshiping from my lesser state.

I refuse to languish.

I make a quilt of Juliet's skin. It sounds gruesome
if you're picturing eye holes and open, empty mouths
all over the place, but it's not like that at all. It's pieced
together in one big pinwheel I learned to make online,
numinous and coruscating like my Pyrex galaxies.

I wear it often.

†

Juliet discovers me one day with the quilt draped over
my shoulders like a cape. She doesn't understand what it
is at first. The realization runs through her face, widening
her eyes into big inky coins and then narrowing them to
angry slits. She yanks her skin off me and throws open the
fire-escape window.

I grab at it as she's straddling the sill. Where the quilt
rips, little white moths flutter out of the fabric, and she
jerks it away from me so hard I stumble back and hit my
head on the metal frame of the futon. I scramble up to
stop her but I'm too late. A breeze blows it into a thousand
shimmery moths—frantic flapping wings and haphazard
turns of flight.

I crumple to the floor as my quilt scatters in the bright
summer sun.

Juliet takes three deep breaths before crossing the
distance between us. She reaches down to me, scowling
as I flinch. She grabs my wrist, pinching the skin between
thumb and forefinger so sharply I try to wrench my arm
from her grip, but her hand holds me firm.

She pulls until my skin tugs away in a thin strip. It
doesn't hurt.

I stop struggling and let my arm hang in the air as she peels it like an apple. At the elbow she uses her teeth to sever the strand.

Underneath I do not look like Juliet. Underneath I am matte and dull, the color of a fetal pig in formaldehyde. I am not surprised.

Juliet's head hangs, slowly shaking.

When she's done collecting her belongings, Juliet says she hopes one day I'll see what she sees, and I can't help but laugh—as if I didn't just watch her realize she's been wasting her time on someone like me.

Alone, I spiral my discarded skin around my arm like a bandage, hiding the regrowth that already stipples my lackluster insides.

Damage Report

Lindsay King-Miller

Incident 26

DEVLIN SLICES TOMATOES for an omelette, fully aware of his own beauty in the golden morning light. It comes as no surprise when Ben sidles up behind him and presses a kiss to the back of his neck. Devlin closes his eyes and leans back into the embrace. In the absence of visual input, he brings the knife down on his fingertips, nearly severing the middle one.

Ben is upset by the blood. Devlin apologizes and cleans it carefully, with bleach. After Ben leaves for work, Devlin detaches the damaged hand and drops it down the biodisposal. The new one is fully regenerated by the time Ben gets home.

Status: Repaired

†

Incident 41

BEN IN THE night, fingers curled into Devlin's hair, gasping
and sweating. They move together in wordless, practiced
ease. Then Ben changes positions without warning, and a
chunk of Devlin's hair comes away in his hand, bloody at
the roots.

"Fuck, Dev, I'm so sorry." He tries to kiss the injured
scalp, but new hair is already growing back.

Status: Repaired

†

Incident 105

"HOW DO YOU expect us to be all right with this?" Ben's
mother says over Thanksgiving turkey. Devlin has been up
all night cooking. "How can we just pretend this is normal?"

"I could have lied to you," Ben says. "You'd never have
known the difference. Can you at least appreciate that
I was honest?" Devlin reaches for his hand to comfort
him, but Ben either doesn't notice or doesn't want to be
comforted.

"So that's it, then? You've just given up on ever finding
a real boyfriend?"

"Goddammit, Devlin *is* my real—"

Later, when his mother is gone, Ben is still for a long
time, muscles standing out in his neck and shoulders.
Then, without warning, he throws a porcelain plate
across the room. It shatters against a wall, spraying shards
everywhere. A sliver of china embeds itself in Devlin's face
just below his left eye.

Status: Repaired.

†

Interior Habitation System Incident 33

BIODISPOSAL AUTOMATION DAMAGED. Incineration cycle
paused pending manual restart.

Status: Unresolved.

†

Incident 154

Devlin runs one damage report after another. No new
incidents. No new incidents. His system is in perfect working
order. He is perfect.

He cannot identify the reason Ben doesn't love him.

He runs damage reports until his CPU freezes. If Ben
got out of bed to check on him, he'd find Devlin sitting in
the living room, apparently paralyzed, moonlight running
down his face like tears. But Ben stays asleep.

Status: System restart. No damage detected.

†

Incident 199

On the bus, paper bags of groceries balanced perfectly
in his lap, Devlin notices a man with thinning blond hair
watching him. He gets off at Devlin's stop and walks
behind him slowly. Devlin has never seen him around the
neighborhood before.

As Devlin puts away eggs and coffee beans, he turns
to see the blond man standing in his kitchen. It's Ben's
kitchen, too, but Ben isn't home. The blond man's face is
red with intent. He pushes Devlin's face into the dining
room table. Devlin has no defensive upgrades.

When he's finished, the man says, "Tell your owner I apologize."

In Devlin's recounting of his day, this detail seems to upset Ben most. "I'm not your fucking owner," he says, and then he sits down on the floor and cries. Devlin carefully removes every part of himself the blond man touched: his cheek, his thighs, the back of his neck. So much regeneration takes a long time. But when he climbs into bed, Ben still won't touch him.

After Ben falls asleep, Devlin doesn't power off like usual. He lies in the dark, listening to a scrabbling sound like rats inside the walls, until his dying battery forces a shutdown.

Status: Repaired.

†

Incident 220

THE SCRATCHING SOUND in the walls gets louder and louder. Ben talks about calling an exterminator. Then, one morning, it's too loud to ignore, and they trace the noise to the biodisposal chute, which has something inside it. Something climbing *up*.

The first thing they see is hands: too many hands, reaching up, grasping for purchase. "What the fuck is that?" Ben asks. Devlin, aware of the distinction between a rhetorical question and a real one, doesn't respond.

The thing that emerges is lumpy and misshapen, vaguely human-shaped, with a thigh where its torso should be. It has hands everywhere, bristling from every corner and joint. Hands with broken fingers or missing nails, hands with gaping holes or ears growing from their palms. A red tongue, blistered and burned, lolls from a toothless mouth. The whole assemblage is knit together with half-healed scars.

It's all Devlin's wounds and mistakes that he's discarded, the pieces that should have burned to ash down there in the dark. Instead they've lived, grown, somehow arranged themselves into a single organism.

The construct has no eyes, but its head tracks from side to side, as though looking from Devlin to Ben and back. Devlin steps in front of Ben to protect him, but Ben pushes him out of the way. He stares at the construct, at its mosaic of injuries, his breath coming fast and shallow. Ben reaches out slowly and brushes his thumb across the construct's ill-fitting face.

Devlin has no protocol for this situation. He has no response to Ben falling to his knees, letting one of those hundred hands caress his hair. "My love," says Ben, tears filling his eyes. "Oh, my love."

Status: No damage detected.

EN EL PATIO DE LA CASA DEL CALLEJÓN

TANIA CHEN

THE HOUSE AT the end of the street has an abandoned fountain on the ground floor patio. It is littered with leaves and bruised flowers, fifty-year-old dust and dirt clogging metal poles that sustain a Statue, lanced through its granite limbs: two arms, a tail and spine.

(It breathes in through stone gills;
behind two sets of eyelids
it flutters its eyes and
breathes out.)

There was, once upon a time, a tree that fed the fountain with oranges and limes. It suckled from infancy the sweet-sour nectars and grew, limbs stretched out like bougainvillaea branches.

There is a man that lives in this house, decayed. Misery and decrepit bones alongside sixty-year-old flaws and fears clog the arteries, that sustain that rickety denture; that creeping heart.

This man hates the Statue; he thrills in its decay and

revels in its abandonment. And so the granite fades under the sun and rain, the pipes rust, flaking off reddish strips as water makes sluggish attempts to circulate.

And the Statue knows it.

It has laid silent for so long, generation after generation. This house is an inheritance, stolen from his sister. Unceremoniously waiting for time to aid his theft, entrenching himself in the bowels of this house: its winding staircase and spacious patio, its wilting garden and decaying Statue.

The dried ink on dotted lines wakes it.

(it breathes in
draws itself upwards,
slinking out of the sea of
leaves
and neglect that has
become its home.)

Behind, it drags its tail; with hands, it claws across the stone, and the yellowed grass, desperate for a taste of clear, cool water. The long metal spikes hold its head, its limbs entrapped. It wails, high pitched and rage-filled.

The Statue loves only women. It remembers this: once upon a time a woman swept the patio—she prayed daily, left flowers and honey, peeled oranges and lit candles. When the grass was green and the trees hung heavy with the fruit of that faded memory, the woman's hair spilled like ink at the edge of the fountain. Her eyes grew marble black and empty as they looked up at the Statue in supplication. She'd always been told that for love to grow it must be cultivated, methodical; this love is not, it is a relentless storm of summer that turns a desert into an ocean.

The Statue remembers the woman with the sweet smile that swept the patio every morning until her brother threw her out and stole everything.

(it drags its tail along the red tiles
of the parlour floor,
past the eyes of other dented statues
that hold the sun and moon.

Up the steps made grey with dust;
  Up along urine stained carpets.
    Up until the velvet red curtain starts—

where it makes its way into the bed
claws curled in the tapestry
claws curled into what lay behind them.)

The man's shock robs him of his voice before the statue collects: his life for all those he ruined. *You're dead,* he says, with no regret and endless resentment, splayed out on the carpet. His head caved in, the sight of the beams in the ceiling fading to black. There is a sound of moving stone, like an avalanche before his world ends.

His last thoughts are of himself, and the bone-deep terror of knowing that the house is no longer his to have. The narrow hallways and secret dining room will belong to his sisters once more.

†

THERE IS A house where a nameless, miserly man no longer lives. Where flowers bloom in season and the sea-salt air permeates through its untamed vine covered gates. The entrance is littered with orange peels, outlining a path to its patio where a fountain sleeps.

At the end of *El Callejon de la Sirena* lies a house thought decayed. A house owned by a statue with a voice of the deep.

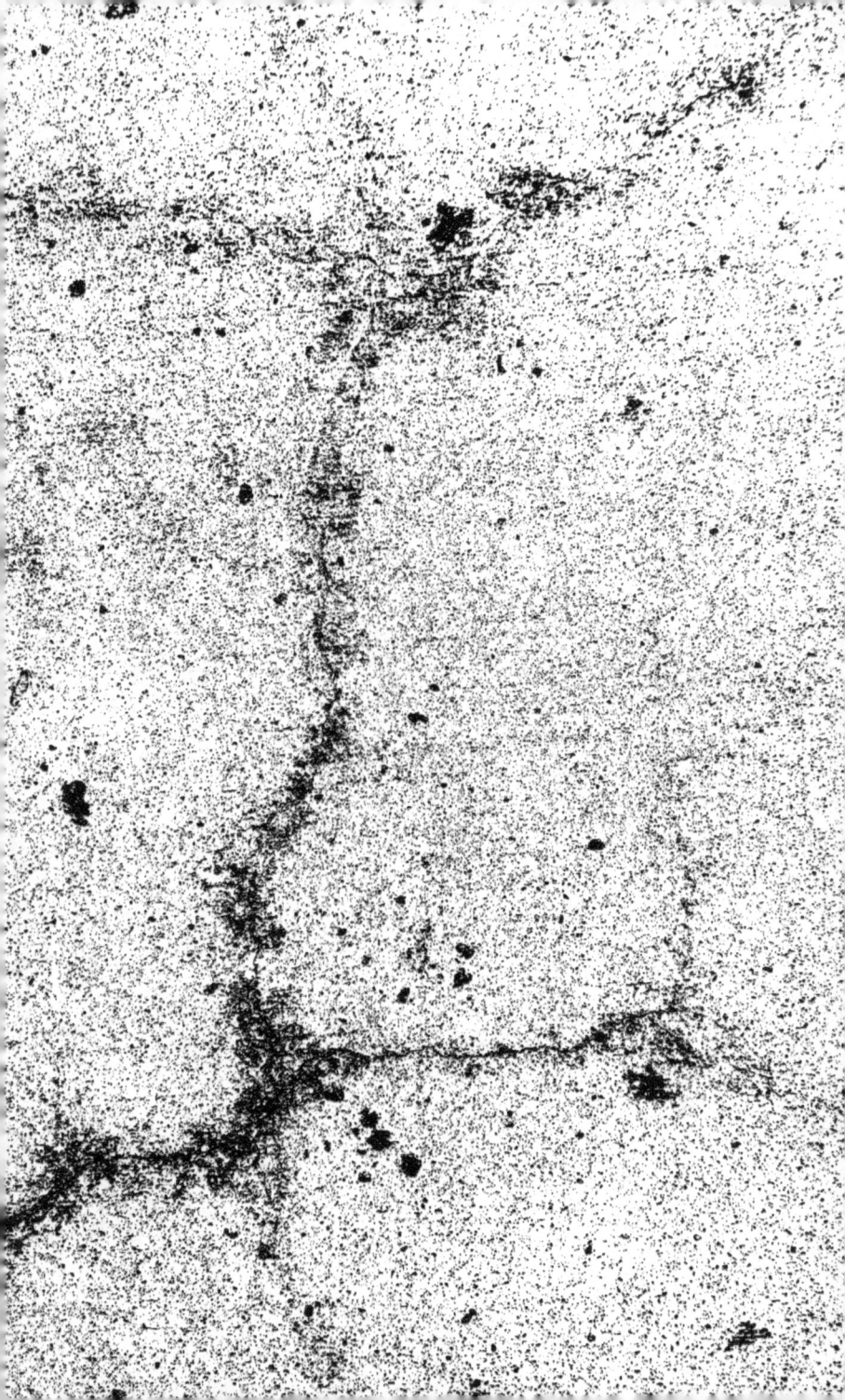

HE KNOWS THAT THE TASTE IS SUCH

Jonathan Louis Duckworth

THE THIRD MORNING of spring, everyone in Mercado gathers in the dusty square, waiting for the Groveman to come for what he's owed. The tinkling of a hundred bells announces the darkly attired Groveman's arrival. Arcadio, a man of twenty springs, can't help but gawk at him with his shoulder-length spill of dark ringlets. Few in Mercado speak of the Groveman willingly, and never do they acknowledge his beauty. Spurs clink from his pointed boots, and tiny silver bells chime from the fringe of his wide, black sombrero. His merest movements occasion delicate music. His handcart is empty of fruit, while the wagon that accompanies him, drawn by an eyeless, wooly beast of six cloven hooves, is laden with the bodies of townsfolk winter stole—the best fertilizer for the grove.

"Now then," the Groveman says, his voice music too. "Where is this year's seed? Who has been dealt the horned snake?"

Everyone is silent when Arcadio lifts his left arm, peels back his sleeve, and reveals the horned serpent—a desiccated thing neither dead nor alive—coiled around his wrist. Everyone except his Mama.

"No! It's not him! Last night, there were no horns on his snake."

"And yet," the Groveman says. That's all.

Mama collapses into sobbing, while Papa stares through Arcadio, uncomprehending. People look at Arcadio with pity or gratitude, while others mutter.

"Where's the beltmaker boy?" the miller whispers.

"It was Weston, he had the horned snake, I saw it," the blacksmith hisses.

"It's me," Arcadio says. "I'm the seed."

The Groveman smiles down on him. "Are you now?"

Now Arcadio walks with the Groveman. Mercado is a dream warbling on the sunset horizon. The snake is gone; unraveled from his wrist and crumbled to dust at a touch of the Groveman's black moleskin glove. No wire or rope or chain binds him to the Groveman, and yet he walks in his shadow through the desert, while the beast and wagon trundle alongside.

"Why did you protect him when he betrayed you?" the Groveman asks.

"I don't know what you mean," Arcadio says. "Your horned snake was dealt me."

"Snakes slither where they will, but I never lose their track."

When his glove cups Arcadio's chin and their eyes lock, Arcadio credits the stories ascribing the Groveman powers of clairvoyance. "Why don't you tell me what really happened, Arcadio?"

†

THE GROVEMAN CAME two days before, as always on the first day of spring, when the last frost melts from the roofs. He came with his handcart full of succulent fruit—skull-sized, with green, waxy rinds guarding sweet custard pitted with black seeds. Arcadio and Weston held hands by the town fence and watched him arrive with the sunrise.

"Why do we put up with him?" Weston asked. "Why every year do we let him have his way? For some fruit?"

"It's always been so."

"But should it be?"

He was always in awe of Weston. No one else in Mercado ever questioned the ways of the world, or the town's tradition. They'd first made love the spring before, when both were sticky with pulp and juice. With a winter spent together they were practically husbands.

"We have no choice. We'd starve without his fruit each year."

"Then why not take it for ourselves?"

Arcadio had no answer.

For all his bold talk, Weston went with Arcadio to claim his fruit, like everyone else. The youngest children were always the first and most enthusiastic to flock to the Groveman's cart. They tore their allotted fruit and buried their faces in the pulp as badland dogs do with carrion. Older children and adults ate with more contemplation, conserving the seeds from which smaller trees might be grown, though these trees would produce an inferior, seedless fruit. But those past their fortieth spring—who could no longer be taken as a seed—ate like the children, with abandon.

At night, the Groveman's bells sang as he set his dried snakes on every doorstep. Morning came and Arcadio found a hornless snake. His relief lasted only as long as it took to find Weston in the beltmaker's workshop. Weston who held a snake with two curved horns on its head. Only Arcadio cried. Weston kept his eyes dry, his voice steady, saying he'd never go with the Groveman.

Three springs back, Harry the fence-painter got the horned snake and ran into the desert, only to be dragged back by a hunting party who delivered him to the

Groveman.

"I'm not going to run. I'm going to kill the Groveman," Weston said. His blue eyes glistened with a terrible conviction, and no argument Arcadio offered could dissuade him. And so it was that Arcadio agreed to help. Weston showed him the tools of his trade—knives for flensing hides, sharp awls that could make holes in leather or gouge eyes.

They sealed their pact with a strong liquor Weston had distilled from pinecones and fruit rinds. After only a few sips, Arcadio's head swam, and he wondered how he'd kill the Groveman with his vision blurred and his limbs numb.

When he awoke, Weston was gone, and Arcadio's snake had been replaced by Weston's horned serpent.

†

"AND STILL YOU protected him," the Groveman says.

They are almost at the grove. Arcadio can see the trees, darker twists of wood set against the evening sky.

"Because I love him."

"Even now?"

"Tell me something. Would it have worked? Could we have killed you?"

The Groveman's bells laugh as he shrugs his head. "I am flesh, like anyone else."

The eyeless beast lows, a sound Arcadio feels in his gut, as they enter the grove. The trees are as tall as they are hideous. Their bark is like oily pitch, and they project at sharp, vertiginous slants from blasted earth heaped with the bones of generations of Mercado's dead. From the trunks, smaller boughs spear out. The seeds of each spring—the sacrifices—hang skewered from these boughs. From them— their bodies retaining their shapes even as they become wooden like the trees—the next years' crop of fruit is already budding.

"Will it hurt, when I'm seeded?"

"I'm sure it does for the chosen. You have a different purpose." He points to the smallest of the trees, from which a familiar shape, shriveled and covered in the oily tar, hangs skewered through his heart. Weston still moves, but the motions are so sluggish it seems more the stubborn memory of life than life itself.

The blue eyes are still open, stark against the tarry sheen of his new skin. Arcadio reaches to ease the lids shut.

The Groveman stands beside him. "No one escapes this, whether chosen as a seed or not. Not the young, nor the old, nor we Grovemen, nor our chosen apprentices. Arcadio. Look up at the trees."

He gazes up and sees his fate in the twisted semblances knotted in the bark. The trunks are their bodies, the boughs their limbs. And the faces—if these are masks of death, then most of the Grovemen died screaming.

The Groveman holds out a tool, something like a gaff, to Arcadio. "Let's begin with the newest start. We'll need to drain the excess sap, or the fruit will sour."

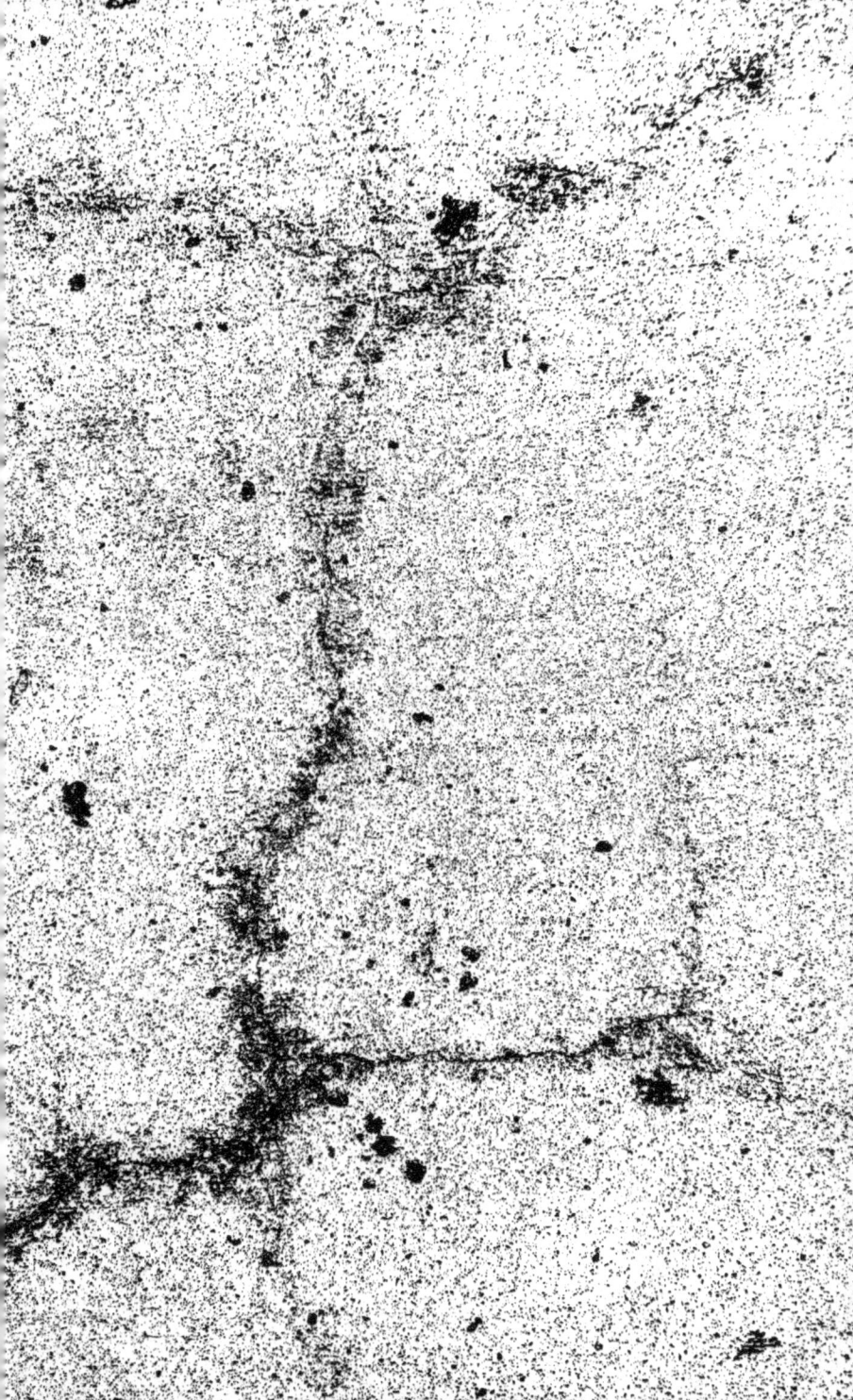

ʄIRST ℋISS

NADIA SHAMMAS

WHEN I FINALLY kissed her, I tasted my own blood. It wasn't fresh. I could taste the grit of sugar from an overly sweet blackberry bramble. I could taste grease from this morning's breakfast. I could taste sour fear. But I couldn't taste her.

It didn't make me want to stop. She was enthusiastic and sloppy, her tongue tracing the outline of my lips before searching the inside of my mouth. I've had people kiss me harder. I've had others knock my teeth with their teeth, or bite my lip too hard, and I bled then, but it didn't feel like this.

I want to lose myself in her frenetic embrace, in this dark room with blasting music and closed eyes, until I am totally consumed by the feeling of her mouth, her skin, her scent. But all I taste is my own blood.

"You're so fucking hot," she murmurs against my cheek. She's pressed all the way against me—fitting her knee between my legs, pushing her breasts against mine, breathing against my sweaty neck—and I am slick all over. I don't just want to touch her—I want to consume her, I want to grind our bones together until there's nothing left of either of us. She's kissing me like she feels the same.

My heart must be pumping, but I don't feel it over the bass of the music. When I was a kid, I'd sit with my bloody noses and swallow any hot blood I could feel welling in my sinus. My teachers told me not to, but I couldn't help it. It was comforting, and it started the bad habit of doing things adults told me not to.

She must have noticed by now? That it's not just sweat, not just saliva, that rusted metal taste, running out of my mouth now, out of her mouth now too. I'm swallowing as much as I can, but she's letting it ooze from between her lips, my bloody spit beginning to pool in the well of her chest. Her tongue slowly glides and presses along my teeth, pushing, like she's looking for something loose. She works my gums until my teeth itch. They feel too tight in my mouth. I squirm in her arms, wheezing as blood leaks out of my nose, covering her dark lips with mealy, viscous warmth. I'm lightheaded, but I'm so close, I'm so close I can feel it and I just need her to push a little further, find that *one spot* and she finds does, it's an incisor it's too tight and relief is right around the bend just please please please

She presses her tongue on that one spot, her knee on the other, and I moan. Really, I gurgle. Back and forth, her tongue tries to loosen it. Agonizingly slow, tantalizingly slow, it's uprooting, pushing against the sweet torn flesh of my mouth like grave dirt. I'm on the edge of it, and then- the sound of suction. A wave of relief takes me, and I come, splattering gore as I cry out. In the final moment, I flick my tongue and shoot the tooth right into the back of her throat. She closes her mouth in surprise.

She pulls back, and we look at each other in the post-kiss clarity. The club is dark, but the reek is impossible to ignore. She's disgusting, covered in blood and slime. She smells like rotten pennies. But then, she smiles at me, jaw clenched tight, her teeth clean and shiny in comparison to the rest of her. She licks her lips and opens her mouth. My tooth, my bloody incisor, sat right in the center of her tongue.

I hold her gaze, hoping she decides to keep me inside her for a long time. Finally, she swallows.

A Table Set
and Waiting

Jordan Shiveley

N o one knows who found the Dark Room first.
Maybe it found us?
Needed us.

We are taught to venerate first times. First time you lose a tooth. First time you taste alcohol. The first time you masturbate through angry tears zipped inside your sleeping bag at a youth group retreat. But even now I only hold the faintest smudge of a memory. A static film of the stairs down to the basement, a slash of yellow flaking paint that peeled away from a door handle, the suffocated rattle and wheeze of an air conditioning ground unit that leaked silent pools over time-polished concrete floor.

The Dark Room.

Even writing it out here, it loses some of the weight that it used to insert on reality. The memory, much like the word, has been erased and rewritten one too many times, its page wearing thin.

†

IT WAS THE summer Colin Haders bit my ear till it bled while I jacked him off in the sweet, musty sweat of the art room's storage closet.

I remember standing in front of the door watching my friends enter it one by one. A glass security door covered with stickers and "No Shoes No Service" and "Bathroom is for customers only" signs this time, but the door itself never mattered. We were there for what was behind it.

Darkness enveloped each of them only a few feet into the room. The darkness did not take them gradually. This was not the receding of a figure slowly being shadowed by distance, time, or the absence of light. It was a sudden swallowing, a working of a throat pulling a mouthful down an esophagus in the space of a breath. A delineated border of dark that pushed across the landscape of their bodies, like thrusting your face into a bathroom sink full of water during a dinner party so no one would hear your choked sobs. One moment they were there, bisected by dirty hallway light and flat impenetrable shadow, and the next they were gone.

It looked so beautiful.

Even in the dim hallway I could still see my skin, my blocky hands scratched from yardwork, my neon blue Swatch watch with the yellow stripes on the band that I said I wore ironically but really I just thought was pretty. My dick was sweaty and hatefully half-hard in my briefs. All the landmarks of polluted meat and bone that served as a trigger for my memories. Remembering the people I wished would want to see me, touch me, spit in my mouth...anything but look at me the way they did in hallways and grocery store lines.

†

ONCE YOU WERE inside, you could look back and see the door floating there. But I never looked back after the first

time. The whole point of the room was what was coming
to meet you in the Dark. The Thing that came forward
slowly, towards your aching, throbbing body of meat
and bones—towards your skin, your fevered needs, your
wrung out dreams. Its approach felt like the change in
air pressure before a storm. The building tension pressed
against your eyeballs and prickled the nape of your neck.

And then it was there.

Always first slithering around your feet, snaking up
along the sweat-lined tender skin at the back of your
knee. Or long bending fingers encircling your ankles and
rubbing back and forth as their grip tightens. I could
never tell what the Thing looked like. In the Dark you
couldn't see shit...that was the point.

Then you feel the claws. Teeth? Knives held by a host
of many small and hungry hands? It didn't matter. They
are tracing over your skin. Pressing through your clothes
to draw a map of what was to come.

†

I WOULD HOLD my breath drawing in gaping mouthfuls
of need. My lungs would burn as I waited for the Thing
to continue. I held so still, afraid if I moved it would dart
away and leave me unfinished and ruined.

When the first cut began, something dry and leathery
would push apart my lips to scrape like rustling paper
through the cage of my teeth. Then talonsknivesteeth
begin to slice along the lines they had been tracing and
the thing in my mouth would push its way further and
further inside of me, filling cavities that I hadn't known
existed until it was inside them. I would of course scream
at this point. I would scream until I felt like every vein
in my body would explode. I would scream up into the
Thing as it entered me, a desperate keening of agony and
welcome.

And then it would all fall away.

The skin. The meat. The time Colin Haders shoved me onto the hard linoleum of the school hallway and broke my glasses just because I leaned against the locker next to his and said "hey you" like a total fucking cum-drunk idiot. The Thing in the Dark would take all of it. After, I would still hear it moving, the slapping sound of meat rearranging itself close and warm; an invisible limb thrusting itself into a wet and welcoming glove. On the floor, free of everything, staring into the blessed Dark as it left in the husk of meat and bones I had entered with.

Sometimes, when it came back, our skins were battered or burned. Alex Caton's was so ruined that he collapsed dead after. We left him in the parking garage and ran. Other times it would drag meat back into the room. Bodies, flensed and broken, joints cracked and bone poking from islands of wet meat like stark white seashells. The Thing wearing my body would stand over me chewing. It sounded more like forcing gristle through a meat grinder than human mastication.

It never let us stay like that. No matter how much we begged or wept. It would always come back and reclothe the blissful nothing it had made of us with the meat and sweat and shame it had taken.

Then it would be done with me, for the time being. Even if I knelt there in the all encompassing dark for hours, it wouldn't return. So I would leave, the weight of my self-perception a raw seeping sunburn against a wool sweater.

Until it became unbearable and I went looking for the Dark Room again.

†

EACH TIME IT took longer and longer to find, until finally it just wasn't there. I can't blame it. I just wish I knew what

I did wrong. What I need to change to be what it wants to consume again.

I never saw what the Thing in the Dark Room looked like

There is a cloudy scratched mirror down here in the basement, hung over a chipped ceramic sink stained from generations of people trying to scrub the world off their skin. When I look at it my face is different. My jaw hangs lower, and when I move it, I can feel the bones in it clicking against each other like the ratcheting of an adjustable wrench, like a chicken bone cracking in the garbage disposal.

I like what I see.

I can feel myself getting hard. I hate it. I hate that I hate it. I rub the corners of my mouth with raspy fingers, letting it stretch open even farther, remembering the razor lines of cuts tracing over me. I think about what it must have looked like, walking around under the sun with my skin taut around it, and I unbutton my pants. I pull my shirt up over my head. The collarbones in the mirror are stark valleys rimmed by freckles. My reflection touches the place Colin Hader marked with his teeth and when it moves my hand away he is still there.

I like what I see.

I stare at my shirt, balled up in my hand, and throw it into the darkness of the basement's far corner, a chumming of the water. I step out of my pants and kick them after it, a baiting of the air. I push my underwear down my hips; my reflection slides one hand over my cock and the other inside my mouth. It probes my teeth, and the thick piece of meat that lies between them vibrates and slides against my stiff fingers as I moan.

I grasp the writhing worm of my tongue hard between two fingers and thumb and squeeze, the loose edges of my mouth shuddering as I scream into my hand. For a moment I think the darkness behind my reflection thickens and my cock jerks of its own accord, but then it is gone.

Come back

The muscles at the root of my tongue spasm but I tighten my grasp. I think about Alex Caton and what was left of him on the floor of the Dark Room—gristle clogging a drain. I think about what the Thing brought back with it, about the wet sound of its feeding. I think about how much of myself I will have to throw into the dark corner of my basement before it notices me again.

I think about my family sleeping upstairs and I pull.

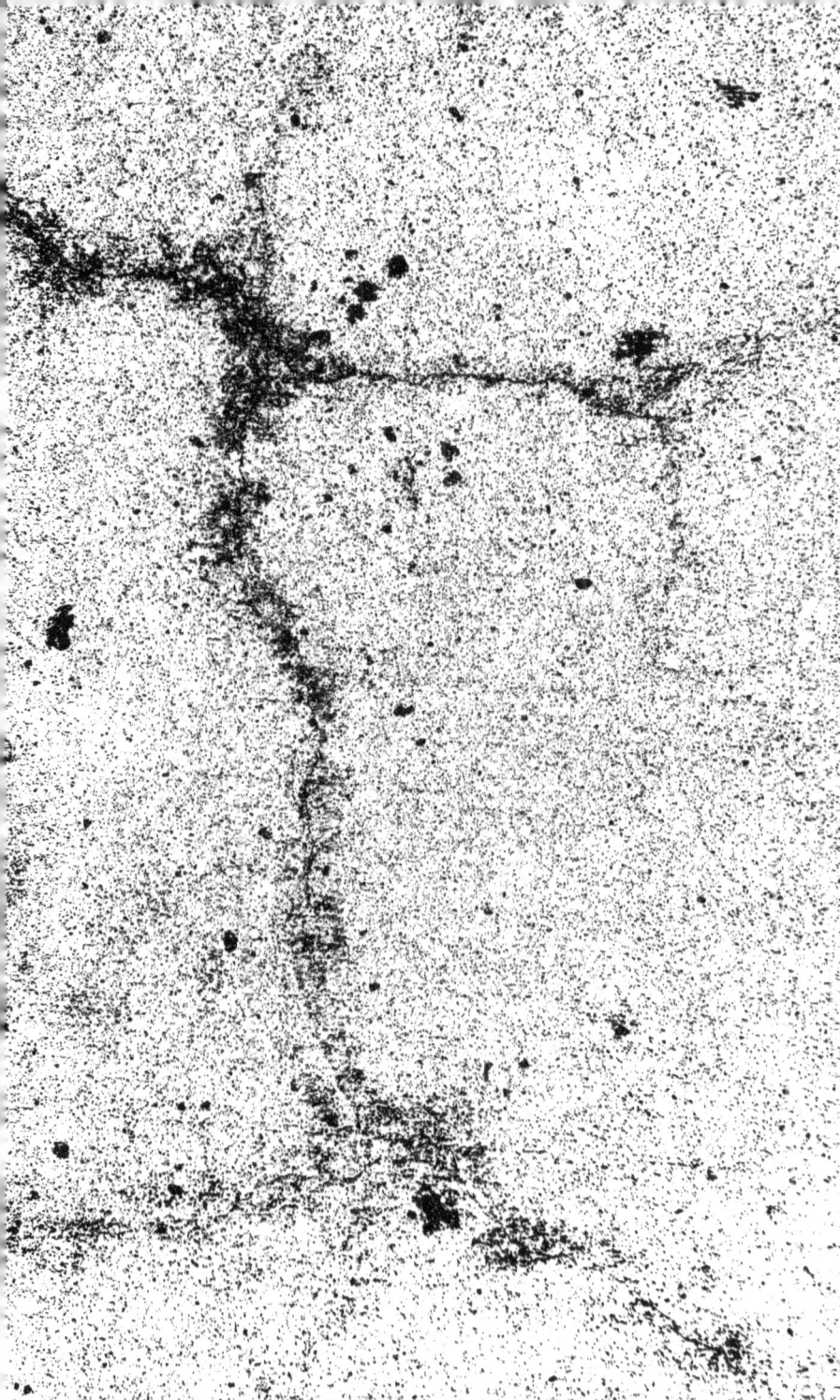

CONTRIBUTORS

Oluwatomiwa Ajeigbe is a writer of the dark and fantastical, a poet, and a reluctant mathematician. He has poetry and fiction published in *F&SF*, *Podcastle*, *Beneath Ceaseless Skies*, *Baffling*, *Lightspeed*, *Anathema Spec*, *FANTASY* and elsewhere. When he's not writing about malfunctioning robots or crazed gods, he can be found doing whatever people do on Twitter at @OluwaSigma. He writes from a room with broken windowpanes in Lagos, Nigeria.

Lauren Bajek is a queer writer, parent, and literary agent living in the Rust Belt. She tweets at @laurenbajek.

E.C. Barrett writes fabulism, folk horror, and dark speculative fiction. They are, or have been, an academic, journalist, bookseller, editor, and linocut artist. A Clarion West graduate, E.C. has words in *Split Lip*, *Strange Horizons*, and elsewhere, and they serve as the book reviews editor for *Reckoning*. E.C. is queer, neurodivergent, and enjoys more maker hobbies than is entirely practical. ecbarrett.com

TJ Berry has been a political blogger, bakery owner, and spent a disastrous two weeks working in a razor blade factory. She now writes science fiction, fantasy, and horror from Los Angeles with considerably fewer on-the-job injuries. Author of *Space Unicorn Blues* and *Five Unicorn Flush*. She's on Twitter @TJBerry.

Sharang Biswas is a writer, artist, and award-winning game designer. He has won IndieCade, ENNIE, and IGDN awards for his games and has showcased interactive works at numerous galleries, museums, and festivals, including

Pioneer Works in Brooklyn, the Institute of Contemporary Art in Philadelphia, and the Museum of the Moving Image in Queens. His nonfiction writing has appeared in publications such as *Dicebreaker, Eurogamer, Unwinnable, First Person Scholar,* and more, while his fiction and poetry has been published by or is forthcoming in *Fantasy, Lightspeed, Strange Horizons,* and more. He is the co-editor of *Honey & Hot Wax: An Anthology of Erotic Art Games* (Pelgrane Press, 2020) and *Strange Lusts / Strange Loves: An Anthology of Erotic Interactive Fiction* (Strange Horizons, 2021). Find him on various social media platforms at @SharangBiswas.

Ryan Breadinc is an up-and-coming writer from Bunbury, Western Australia. A self-proclaimed mess of a human being, he's found his passion in writing the weirdest shit he can come up with at the time, and then bullying his friends into reading it. (Just kidding.) You can find him rambling about half-baked ideas for his next story on social media at @breadincbooks, or in his office with a few birds yelling at him for attention as he tries desperately to get some work done.

Tania Chen is a Chinese-Mexican queer writer. Their work has been published in *Unfettered Hexes* by Neon Hemlock. They are also a first reader for *Strange Horizons* and *Nightmare Magazine* and a graduate of the Clarion West Novella Bootcamp workshop of January/Feb 2021. Their work is upcoming in *Pleiades Magazine, Strange Horizon* and *Baffling.*

Sean Chua is controlled by a swarm of tiny amoebas which have taken residence in his brain. He cannot write for very long because the amoebas are very small. His interests are urban affects, strange bodies, and tap water. He tweets as @anafabulic.

Georgia Cook is an illustrator and writer from London. She has written for publications such as *Baffling, Vastarien Lit,* and *Flame Tree Press,* as well as the Doctor Who range with Big Finish. She frequently writes and narrates for horror anthology podcasts such as *Creepy, The Other Stories,* and *The Night's End,* and has written for numerous webcomics. She can be found on twitter at @georgiacooked and on her website at georgiacookwriter.com.

Karyn De Freitas is a writer, scholar, activist, and part-time jumbie from Trinidad and Tobago. They have been published in *Eye to the Telescope* and *FIYAH Literary Magazine of Black Speculative Fiction.* Follow them on Twitter @pandaraUwU.

Jonathan Louis Duckworth is a completely normal, entirely human person with the right number of heads and everything. He received his MFA from Florida International University and his PhD from University of North Texas. He is the author of *Have You Seen the Moon Tonight? & Other Rumors* (JournalStone Publishing) and his speculative fiction work appears in *Pseudopod, Fantasy & Science Fiction, Beneath Ceaseless Skies, Southwest Review,* and elsewhere. He is an active HWA member.

Louis Evans is neither the depressed goth twink boyfriend, nor the levelheaded blond bear boyfriend, but some sort of unholy hybrid between the two. His work has appeared in *Vice, F&SF, Nature: Futures,* and elsewhere. He lives with his spouse and two cats named after fictional detectives.

Stephen Granade is a physicist, writer, and editor from Huntsville, Alabama, the city with a Saturn V rocket in its skyline. Their stories have appeared in *Escape Pod* and *Podcastle.* Their game, *Professor of Magical Studies,* is available from Choice of Games, and they co-edit *Small Wonders,* a speculative flash fiction and poetry magazine.

Ruth Joffre is the author of the story collection *Night Beast.* Her work has been shortlisted for the Creative Capital Awards, longlisted for The Story Prize, and supported by residencies at the Virginia Center for the Creative Arts, Lighthouse Works, and The Arctic Circle. Her writing has appeared or is forthcoming in more than 50 publications, including *Lightspeed, Nightmare, Fantasy, TriQuarterly, Pleiades, Reckoning,* and the anthologies *Unfettered Hexes: Queer Tales of Insatiable Darkness* and *2022 Best of Utopian Speculative Fiction.* A graduate of Cornell University and the Iowa Writers' Workshop, Ruth served as the 2020 - 2022 Prose Writer-in-Residence at Hugo House. She was a Visiting Writer at University of Washington Bothell and George Mason University in 2023.

Shingai Njeri Kagunda is an Afrosurreal/futurist storyteller from Nairobi, Kenya with a Literary Arts MFA from Brown. She has work in or upcoming in *Omenana, Fantasy magazine, FracturedLit, Khoreo, Africa Risen,* and *Uncanny Magazine.* Her debut novella *& This is How to Stay Alive* was published by Neon Hemlock Press in October 2021. She is the co-editor of *Podcastle Magazine* and the co-founder of Voodoonauts. Shingai is a creative writing teacher, an eternal student, and a lover of all things soft and Black.

Lindsay King-Miller is the author of *Ask a Queer Chick: A Guide to Sex, Love, and Life for Girls who Dig Girls* (Plume, 2016). Her fiction has appeared in *The Fiends in the Furrows* (Nosetouch, 2018), *Tiny Nightmares* (Catapult, 2020), *Planet Scumm, Fireside,* and numerous other publications. Her first novel *The Z Word,* about a zombie outbreak at a small-town Pride festival, will be published by Quirk Books in May 2024. She lives in Denver, CO with her partner and their two children.

Kristen Koopman is a graduate student, writer, and nerd. Her interests include blatant escapism, overanalyzing anything and everything, playing with her dog, and enough garlic to kill vampires at twenty paces. She is definitely not two smaller Kristen Koopmans in a trenchcoat.

Iori Kusano is a queer Asian American writer and Extremely Ordinary Office Gremlin living in Tokyo. They are a graduate of Clarion West 2017. Their novella *Hybrid Heart* is available from Neon Hemlock Press, and their short fiction appears in various magazines. Find them on Twitter @IoriKusano and Instagram as iori_stagram, or at kusanoiori.com.

Ann LeBlanc is a writer, editor, and woodworker. Her stories can be found in *Clarkesworld, Escape Pod, Apparition Lit,* and on the lips of the dead. Her debut novella, *The Transitive Properties Of Cheese*, is forthcoming from Neon Hemlock Press in 2024. Ann is also the editor of *Embodied Exegesis*, an anthology of transfemme cyberpunk stories by transfemme authors (out in 2024). You can find her online at www.annleblanc.com

Gerri Leen lives in Northern Virginia and originally hails from Seattle. In addition to being an avid reader, she's passionate about horse racing, tea, and collecting encaustic art and raku pottery. She has work appearing in *The Magazine of Fantasy & Science Fiction, Nature, Strange Horizons, Deep Magic*, and others. She's edited several anthologies for independent presses, is finishing some longer projects, and is a member of SFWA and HWA. See more at gerrileen.com.

Born and raised in Stockholm, Sweden, **Emma Lindhagen** is a queer speculative fiction writer. They have self-published three novellas as well as myriad flash fiction pieces on their website. When they aren't writing, Emma enjoys making lists and trying to learn a slightly unrealistic number of new languages. Emma has a penchant for tea, whiskey, chocolate, bubble baths, the color purple and the music of Leonard Cohen. They currently live in Stockholm with a long-time partner.

AJ Lucy is a fiction writer who lives with her wife in Philadelphia. She has a BA in fine arts and a PhD in molecular biology. In her spare time she fosters sick cats and helps organize the Alpha Young Writers Workshop for teens interested in creating all kinds of speculative fiction.

Jackson Jesse Nash (he/him) is a trans writer from Essex, England. His fiction and poetry have appeared in *Channel, Rattle, TypeHouse Literary Magazine, Impossible Archetype* and others. In 2020 he was shortlisted for the Creative Future Writer's Award. Jackson is a fellow of the Lambda Literary Retreat, and has been selected for the Next Up 2022 writer's development programme. He has a PhD in Gender Studies with a thesis on trans representation in YA. He lives in Brighton with his partner and their Maine coon.

Miyuki Jane Pinckard is a writer, game designer, researcher, and educator. Her fiction can be found in *Strange Horizons, Uncanny Magazine, Flash Fiction Online*, and other venues. She was born in Tokyo, Japan and now lives in Venice, California, with her partner and a little dog. She likes wine and mystery novels and karaoke. Follow her @miyukijane and at www.miyukijane.com.

Fruzsina Pittner is a designer, illustrator and writer currently on loan in the Scottish games industry. She is a serial committer of yarn crimes, has a fondness for hills that are really good and round, and has been known to enjoy sticking her hands into dirt. She has sworn off social media, but can be found on her website fruzsipittner.com.

Arden Powell is an author and illustrator from the Canadian East Coast. A nebulous entity, they live with a small terrier and an exorbitant number of houseplants, and have conversations with both. They write many flavours of speculative fiction, and everything they write is queer. They can be found on twitter @ArdenPowell, or on their blog at ardenpowell.wordpress.com.

Perry Ruhland is a writer and filmmaker based in Chicago, Illinois. His work focuses on grotesque terrors, gay masculinities, and cosmic despair.

Nadia Shammas is a queer Palestinian-American author and game developer from Brooklyn, now living in Toronto, Canada. She's best known for her speculative work in comics and prose, primarily *Squire*, a YA Middle Eastern fantasy graphic novel co-created with Sara Alfageeh. Their credits include *Strange Horizons, Vastarien*, and most recently, their eldritch horror graphic novel *Where Black Stars Rise* (co-created with Marie Enger) won a 2023 Ignyte Award. Nadia particularly loves working with body horror, hauntings, and the uncanny. When not writing, she attempts to win the love of her cats, Lilith and Dash.

Jordan Shiveley is the author of the Dread Singles (@hottestsingles) Twitter account. Their work has also been seen in a variety of short fiction collections and tabletop roleplaying games, the *Old Gods of Appalachia* and *Caring Into the Void* podcasts, as well as the upcoming novel *Hot Singles in Your Area* from Unbound. They live and work in Minneapolis, Minnesota. More at jordanshiveley.com

Bogi Takács (e/em/eir/emself or they pronouns) is a Hungarian Jewish agender trans person and an immigrant to the US. E is a winner of the Lambda award for editing *Transcendent 2: The Year's Best Transgender Speculative Fiction*, the Hugo award for Best Fan Writer, and a finalist for other awards. Eir second short story collection *Power to Yield and Other Stories* is coming in 2024 from Broken Eye Books. You can find Bogi talking about books at www.bogireadstheworld.com, and on various social media like Mastodon, Bluesky, Patreon and Instagram as bogiperson.

About Baffling Magazine

Baffling Magazine is a quarterly online magazine of flash fiction that publishes fantasy, science fiction & horror stories with a queer bent. Stories are first shared online with our patrons throughout the year. If you'd like to support us, please visit patreon.com/neonhemlock.

Visit us online at bafflingmag.com and on Twitter at @bafflingmag.

About the Press

Neon Hemlock is a Washington, DC-based small press publishing speculative fiction, rad zines and queer chapbooks. We punctuate our titles with oracle decks, occult ephemera and literary candles. Publishers Weekly once called us "the apex of queer speculative fiction publishing" and we're still beaming.

Learn more about us at neonhemlock.com and on Twitter at @neonhemlock.